But he followed along behind, laughing a little at Old-Man's clumsy
climbing

KOOTENAI WHY STORIES

BY

FRANK B. LINDERMAN

[CO–SKEE–SEE–CO–COT]

Illustrated by
CHARLES LIVINGSTON BULL

Introduction to the Bison Books Edition
by Celeste River

THE AUTHORIZED EDITION

University of Nebraska Press
Lincoln and London

⊛ The paper in this book meets the minimum requirements of American National Standard for Information Sciences—Permanence of Paper for Printed Library Materials, ANSI Z39.48-1984.

First Bison Books printing: 1997
Most recent printing indicated by the last digit below:
10   9   8   7   6   5   4   3   2   1

Library of Congress Cataloging-in-Publication Data
Linderman, Frank Bird, 1869–1938.
Kootenai why stories / by Frank B. Linderman (Co-skee-see-co-cot); illustrated by Charles Livingston Bull; introduction to the Bison Books edition by Celeste River.—Authorized ed.
    p.   cm.
Originally published: New York: C. Scribner's Sons, 1926.
Includes bibliographical references (p.).
ISBN 0-8032-7972-8 (pbk.: alk. paper)
1. Kutenai Indians—Folklore. 2. Tales—Montana.   I. River, Celeste.   II. Title.
E99.K85L5   1998
338.2'089'973—dc21   97-25922
                                                                       CIP

Reprinted from the original 1926 edition by Charles Scribner's Sons, New York.

INTRODUCTION TO THE BISON BOOKS EDITION

Celeste River

These are told in the Indian's own words as nearly as possible
and the effect is of listening to the story teller himself before a
blazing camp-fire in some remote trading post.
> —*Saturday Review of Literature,* 27 November 1926

When Frank Bird Linderman wrote *Kootenai Why Stories* in
1925, forty years had passed since he first arrived in the land of
the Kootenai Indians. Born in Ohio in 1869, he had journeyed
from the Midwest to the Flathead Valley in northwestern Montana Territory in March 1885. In later years he reminisced, "I
came to Montana when I was a boy and Fortune directed my
way to its wildest portion, the Flathead country, where I trapped
and hunted for nearly seven years. During all of this time I was
among the Flatheads and Kootenais."

The first Indian he encountered was a Flathead warrior named
Red-horn, who instinctively knew that he was a rank pilgrim.
"His smile said as plainly as words that he thought me a babe in
the woods." When they met at Linderman's camp in the forest,
Red-horn, who became a lasting friend, tried through sign language to impress upon the young novice that he was a Flathead,
not a Kootenai. In the fall of 1885 thirty lodges of refugee
Chippewa and Cree Indians, who had come over the "medicine-
line" after taking part in the Riel Rebellion in Canada, camped
near Linderman in the Flathead Valley. Some were still wounded
from the fighting, and he helped them hunt for meat. "I had had
trouble with the Kootenai," he wrote, "so I sought to strengthen
the friendship between the new arrivals and myself."

Linderman explained this concern about the Kootenais in his memoirs, *Montana Adventure*, written in 1929 and 1930: "The Kootenais, or Kootenahha, as they call themselves, resented the settling of the Flathead country by white men, and I began to hear stories of missing trappers. . . . We used no horse bells, avoided Indian camps, and were careful with our campfires." Sometimes Linderman hunted and trapped alone in the mountains; at other times he had partners, some of them Indians. Men with names like Red Abbot, Jack Bartlett, Hank Jennings, Black George, Left-hand (Dominick), Baptiste, and Koonsaw. Despite knowing many Indians well, he had several tense encounters with Kootenais while camping alone in the wilds.

There were Canadian Kootenais camped in the northern Flathead Valley and at the head of Flathead Lake, while a band of American Kootenais were living on the west side of the lake on the Flathead Reservation, which was established by the Hellgate Treaty in 1855 for the Flathead, Kootenai, and Upper Pend d'Oreille Indians. According to ethnographer Harry Turney-High, this group, the Somers-Dayton-Elmo band, was founded from the Libby-Jennings band of Kootenai, which is "the most recent in origin of all the old bands."

The leader of this band was Chief Aeneas Paul, whose mother was a Kootenai named One Hoof (later Mary) and whose father was an Iroquois named Ignace Big Knife, who had come to the Northwest many years before, probably in the employment of the Hudson's Bay Company. According to Linderman, "Aeneas, or Big Knife, the old chief of the Kootenais, . . . was a strong man, and at least twice held his people in check when the young bloods among them were clamoring for revenge against the white settlers in Flathead valley, [who had killed his son]. Even then, when he must have found it difficult to control his own wrath, he counselled peace, and smothering his pride, held the Kootenai tribe from running amuck."

During the period from 1887 to 1890, a number of grievous incidents occurred in the Flathead area when the murders of white men were discovered by local settlers, and the supposed perpetrators were caught and hung at the town of Demersville on the Flathead River. "Unproved stories of killings persisted until all trappers looked upon the Kootenais as enemies," Linderman wrote. "No doubt there was truth in some of these tales, and I believe that there was some bushwhacking on both sides."

In 1889 Montana became a state, and in the fall of 1892 Linderman left the Flathead country. "Many a day I had hunted with the Crees and Chippewas," he reminisced in *Montana Adventure*. "I had many friends among the Blackfeet and Flatheads, and even a few Kootenais called me 'friend.'" He subsequently became an assayer, miner, newspaper owner, state legislator, assistant secretary of state, and state agent for an insurance company. In 1908 he spearheaded an eight-year effort to acquire a reservation for the landless Chippewas and Crees he had known in the Flathead, becoming in the process an outspoken advocate of religious freedom for the American Indian.

Linderman's first book, *Indian Why Stories*, a compilation of Chippewa, Cree, and Blackfeet legends, was published in 1915. With plans to pursue his newfound literary career, he retired in 1917 on savings from his insurance business, and moved his family from Helena, the state capital, to a secluded log home at Goose Bay on the west shore of Flathead Lake. "I feel bound to save the life of the old Northwest as I saw it," he wrote. "I want very much to not only tell the story of this country but to keep straight its history, and whatever I do will always bear light on these points, so help me, the shades of men I knew here."

Because their environment was totally different from that of the plains Indians, their legends are distinctively their own and very different from those of other tribes.
—*New York Times Book Review*, 5 December 1926

To all who have tried to study them, the Kootenais are an enigmatic people. At the time of first contact in the 1790s, they were hunters and gatherers living in semi-nomadic bands around Kootenay Lake and the headwaters of the Kootenai and upper

Columbia rivers in eastern British Columbia, western Montana, and northern Idaho. Historical records show over seventy ways to spell the word *Kootenai*, used to name many geographical features and places in their traditional homeland, and yet little is known about Kootenai prehistory. Migration myths are scarce in their oral tradition. Although a few stories indicate a time when they may have lived on the other side of the mountains, most of their legends center in the "Big Village" in the Tobacco Plains area, at the border between British Columbia and Montana, which led Turney-High to conclude that Tobacco Plains is where the Kootenais "woke-up."

Though some of their cultural traits, myths, and legends bear similarities to Plains and Plateau cultures, the Kootenais developed unique adaptations to their semi-isolated geographic area. Their language is an isolate, unlike that of any of their neighbors. Linguists have not been able to place them clearly in a language stock or category with any other North American tribes.

They fished with lines, traps, weirs, and spears, a pursuit that distinguished them from the Plains Indians, who had a taboo against fishing; they also went on communal bison hunts to the plains, even crossing the Rocky Mountains in midwinter to "go to buffalo." Showshoes were used to traverse their mountainous terrain in winter, and canoes were used to navigate the many lakes and rivers of their intermountain homeland. Some bands made lodges of bark or plant fibers, like those of the Plateau Indians; others lived in skin tipis like those used on the Great Plains. They practiced the annual Sun Dance, a ritual associated with Plains cultures; yet Linderman noted that "the frog, never figuring in the stories of the plains' Indian, is a leading character in Kootenai tales."

In his preface to *Kootenai Why Stories* Linderman said he had learned from his trapper associates that "*Kootenai*, or *Kutenai*, or *Kootenaha* (as they call themselves), meant 'Flatbow' or 'Flat-bow-people,'" but he never found a member of the tribe who could or would translate the word into English. "The name 'Flat-bows' may have been only epithetical and familiar to those who knew them," he wrote. "The Flathead call the Kootenai *Cus-sun-ga* [Ksanka], which means 'an arrow sticking straight up in the ground.'" Plains Indians made the signs "Whitetail-deer-people" in naming the Kootenai, Linderman said, and when naming themselves in sign-language the Kootenai made the signs "Whitetail-deer-robe-people" or "Buckskin-robes."

The Kootenais were noted for the quality and beauty of their tanned hides. Turney-High said they "considered the preparation of hides, especially for clothing, a high art." They used white clay to treat soiled hides and "were proud of having spotless, white skin clothing." Living in an abundant world with so many types of animals, they were able to assign special uses to the hides of different species. In fact, Turney-High wrote that "the Kutenai considered their land a fortunate one wherein any industrious man could get plenty to eat for himself and family."

In contrast to this, an anecdote that Linderman wrote from his home at Goose Bay in November 1920 reveals the plight that had befallen the Montana Kootenai: "An old Indian pitched his lodge on the place the other day and killed two nice bucks—then, when he went away, I noticed a good pair of overalls that he had given to the Sun. It's a mark of hard times when a Kootenai gives clothes to the Sun just for luck enough to kill two deer."

Linderman, too, was looking on hard times. His savings were running low. But when a friend offered him employment in 1922 he answered: "I have long ago determined that there are more worthwhile things than dollars. . . . I feel it a duty to, in some way, preserve the old West, especially Montana, in printers' ink."

> There is a fine ring of reality to them and a simplicity and
> vigor that makes them unusual among the group of Indian and
> folk legends written down second-hand.
> —*Saturday Review of Literature,* 27 November 1926

While Linderman was learning firsthand about the life and legends of the Indians, in 1891 anthropologists Franz Boas and

Alexander Chamberlain were separately collecting stories from Kootenai informants. Years later Boas compiled *Kutenai Tales*, a report that included many of these legends, for the Bureau of American Ethnology. In summarizing his findings he concluded that "one of the most characteristic traits of Kutenai folk tales is the systematic development of animal society."

Archetypes of most of the stories and animal characters in Linderman's narrative, *Kootenai Why Stories*, are easily found in the texts of Boas's scientific report, but the resemblance stops there. *Kutenai Tales* consists of phonetic transcriptions and word-by-word translations of the stories. Also, Chamberlain's notes were brief and fragmentary because it was his first field expedition and, Boas said, "it requires a considerable amount of practice to record long tales." By contrast, after years of practice as a recorder of Indian legends and as a storyteller himself, Linderman's retelling of the Kootenai myths and legends are rich with contextual imagery. His mastery of sign-language, his knowledge of woodcraft and experience in the great out-of-doors, and his genuine respect for the Indians' spiritual beliefs give an unparalleled dimension to Linderman's rendering of these oral narrations.

Literary critic and fellow author Fredric F. Van de Water, who knew Linderman well, wrote in 1939, "He spoke straight, with tongue or pen. . . . and because of his approach, which was simple and earnest and abidingly friendly . . . a suspicious people completely trusted him." In *Kootenai Why Stories*, the opening to "*Old*-man and the Thunder-birds" reveals Linderman's understanding of that sacred trust, as well as the subtlety of his literary skill: "'The white frost has come,' said Two-comes-over-the-hill, drawing his robe about his aged shoulders. '*Old*-man has painted the leaves, and they will soon dance with the North Wind. The season when the Thunder-birds visit us has gone. They will come no more until the leaves are green again.'"

We see here Linderman's respect for native tradition and propriety, keeping in mind a passage by Barre Toelken: "Coyote stories must be told only after the first killing frost and before the first thunderstorm—that is, in wintertime as defined by nature itself." (Coyote is Skinkoots in Kootenai stories.) Also found in Linderman's writing is an important element of style that conveys a sense of the live context of the original stories, an element identified by Toelken as "a sense of locality, a feeling for place—both geographic and sacred."

Linderman loved the natural world of the Kootenias: "the deep forests, the rugged mountains, the clear lakes, and swift-running streams of the great Northwest, . . . in all the world there is no country more beautiful,than this." He knew well the habits of the many birds and animals of the forest. In the early days the Chippewas and Crees called him *Sings-like-a-bird*, and old Kootenais called him *Bird-singer*. Attuned with this sensitivity, he draws us into the landscape of the stories themselves.

In the opening to *Kootenai Why Stories*, we follow as his friend Walks-in-the-water takes him to the lodge of Two-comes-over-the-hill. It is night, the usual time for telling stories. It is October; frost has turned the larch needles golden. The trail through the shadowy forest feels soft beneath our feet. We hear the waves at the edge of the lake, we see the moonlight on its surface, we smell the smoke of the lodge-fire. The stage is set, our senses are engaged, we are in the present.

The reader enters the immediacy of the storytelling event, imagining the ambiance within the lodge of Two-comes-over-the-hill. We are reminded of the weather outside, the warmth of the fire, the hoot of the owl, *Co*-pee, whose voice—"deep and clear in the keen air"—sounds very close. We wait, with the children, as the old man pauses to smoke his pipe. We learn to listen. We hear the Great Stillness.

The year 1926 was a significant one for Linderman, who was then in the midst of his literary career. In January, upon learning that Charles Scribner's Sons planned to publish *Kootenai Why Stories*, he wrote of his books, "They have saved a small portion of the life of the old Northwest as I first saw it, and of this I am proud."

Two-comes-over-the-hill, the Kootenai storyteller, circa 1925.
Courtesy K. Ross Toole Archives, University of Montana.

That summer he went to the Crow reservation to gather stories for *Old Man Coyote*. By early October *Kootenai Why Stories* had been released, then later that month he felt the loss of his long-time friend, Charley Russell, who had illustrated his first two books of Indian legends, and had often gone on camping trips with him in Kootenai country. As compatriots they had shared a purpose in life: to describe the Old West in true colors—one with paint, the other in printer's ink.

In a November review of *Kootenai Why Stories* western author Mary Austin wrote, "There is a flowing movement in the narration, such as is rarely absent from authentic primitive Tellings." Linderman's works do speak with an authentic voice. In June 1927 he received an honorary Doctor of Letters degree from The University of Montana for his literary works and his research in the field of Indian customs, beliefs, and traditions.

The lasting quality of those works and the respectful detail of that research are evident throughout the pages of *Kootenai Why Stories*. In this book, Linderman's sense of duty was fulfilled. A portion of the old Northwest, as seen through Kootenai eyes, is preserved.

SOURCES

Reminiscences about Linderman's early days in the Flathead are from his memoirs, *Montana Adventure* (1985), and a letter in the Linderman Estate files. Facts about Kootenais in the Flathead area in the late 1880s were found in the Samuel E. Johns Papers (K. Ross Toole Archives, University of Montana, Missoula) and Harry Holbert Turney-High's "Ethnography of the Kutenai" (1941).

General information on the Kootenais is derived from Alexander Francis Chamberlain's "Report on the Kootenay Indians of South-Eastern British Columbia" (1893); Chamberlain's "The Kootenay Indians" (1906); "The Kutenai" in volume 7 of Edward S. Curtis's *The North American Indian* (1911); and Cynthia Manning's thesis at the University of Montana, "An

Ethnohistory of the Kootenai Indians" (1983). Franz Boas's *Kutenai Tales* (1918) provides some of the earliest known recorded texts of Kootenai stories.

Linderman's statements about writing and about his books are from letters in the Frank Bird Linderman Papers (K. Ross Toole Archives). His anecdote on "a mark of hard times" is from a letter in a privately held collection. About the frog, names for the Kootenai, and the beauty of their natural world, see Linderman's preface to *Koottenai Why Stories* (1926); about the Thunder-birds, going to the lodge of Two-comes-over-the-hill, and the sense of nearness of *Co*-pee, see *Kootenai Why Stories* (1997).

Frederic Van de Water's eulogy, "The Work of Frank B. Linderman," is found in *Frontier and Midland* (spring 1939). The Barre Toelken quotations are from his foreword in *Giving Birth to Thunder, Sleeping with His Daughter: Coyote Builds North America*, by Barry Lopez (1990). Mary Austin is quoted from a book review in the *New Republic*, 10 November 1926. On Linderman's Doctor of Letters degree, see *Montana Adventure*.

Facts about the Kootenai were verified in a personal visit with elders of the Standing Arrow band at the Kootenai Cultural Center in Elmo, Montana, on 20 January 1997, and in phone conversations with the Cultural Center's director in March 1997.

CONTENTS

ILLUSTRATIONS

INTRODUCTION

"*Su-ap'-pe*, Whiteman, if you would listen to Kootenai tales of *Old*-man, come with me. I will take you to the lodge of Two-comes-over-the-hill. His lodge is tall and white with a smoky top, and it stands to-night alone under the moon by the lapping waters of Flathead Lake.

"The Great Stillness is there, *Su-ap'-pe*. And yet there are noises. But these only make the Stillness deeper. When the noises come you will listen. When they are gone you will listen until they come again. It is while one waits for the noises that the Stillness is deepest. Then it is like a soft robe about him, and his heart sings. At first there will be only the lapping of the waters — lapping, lapping, as though little children were playing. Then far out on the dark lake, where the waves reach far but touch nothing, the Spotted Loon will laugh, and the Gray Goose will gonk at the light in the white lodge of Two-comes-over-the-hill.

"These are the noises that are in the Great Stillness, *Su-ap'-pe*. Will you come?"

Walks-in-the-water was my friend. He was old and wrinkled, and much respected by his people, the Kootenais. His presence would insure me a welcome in the lodge of Two-comes-over-the-hill, where I knew the old Medicine-man was telling stories to his grandchildren.

"Yes, I will go with you, Walks-in-the-water," I said gladly; and he led the way.

The air was keen. The full October moon was working its wonders among the tall larch-trees. Already the frost had colored their needles, and they were falling thick upon the ground. The trail, soft as velvet beneath our feet, was carpeted with them, and in the silvery light it resembled a golden ribbon winding through a world inhabited only by shadows. And how softly the old Indian walked; and how like a *shadow*, himself, moving among the stationary thousands cast down by the larches!

At last we left the larch-trees, and then, as though to show its most secret places, the trail led us through dense fir thickets, dark and fragrant under the moon. And here — twice, out of the deeper shadows that hid them — frightened deer bounded away, their tails waving and bobbing like white linen handkerchiefs, before we came to the pine-trees that skirted the lake.

Their huge trunks and silent tops, decently apart on the gentle slope of the hillside, reminded me of an army of giants commissioned by some pagan god to guard his secrets from such as I, and, looking down, I was conscious of a feeling of intrusion. I saw the water flashing in the moonlight, heard a grebe call plaintively as though in protest against my coming, and then I saw a blurred light, and smelled woody smoke. We had come to the lodge of Two-comes-over-the-hill.

INTRODUCTION

"How!" said Walks-in-the-water, raising the door, as though of right.

"How! How!" greeted the old Medicine-man, hastening to fill his black stone pipe that he might offer it as a testimonial of his joy at our visit.

Walks-in-the-water told him why we had come, and then, as soon as the pipe had been passed, the old Medicine-man put wood on his fire.

Smilingly, he turned to his grandchildren, on whose faces there had been keen disappointment when we entered, and resumed his story.

KOOTENAI WHY STORIES

I

WHY SKINKOOTS'S ARMS ARE THIN

*Y*AH–CASSIN–KIN–NAH–WASKA (the Almighty) made *Nu-la-kin-nah* (*Old*-man). Then *Nu-la-kin-nah* (*Old*-man) made this world, and all that is on it.

At first all the animals and birds were Persons. They were not People. They were only *Persons*. *Old*-man made them that way at first. He changed some of them himself when they did not suit him. War changed others, while some changed their looks and even their habits for themselves, as I will tell you.

When the world was young and the animals and birds were *Persons*, *Old*-man was their Chief. He had to live with *somebody*, and there were no other People on the world, so that he was obliged to live with these *Persons* he had made, or live alone.

1

Like *Old*-man, many of these *Persons* knew magic. Their Medicine was strong, and they did many strange things, as you shall see. But all had to learn before they became wise, for this world was young, and no Person knew how best to get along here.

First of all, *Old*-man made Skinkoots, the Coyote, the smart Person. You hear him every night in the forest. His voice is the same to-day as it was when the world was young. But he has changed many of his ways. He had to. He kept poking his nose into the business of the other Persons until finally he got into trouble. The trouble changed Skinkoots, as I will tell you. Of course it would not have happened if Skinkoots had listened to *Nu-la-kin-nah*, *Old*-man. But he did not listen, and now his legs are skinny. Yes, and they are homely legs, too. But it takes a smart Person to fool Skinkoots to-day.

Listen! The day was fine. *Old*-man was walking in the forest. He was trying to find some Person to talk to. He could hear Persons, sometimes, but they always moved before he got near enough to speak to them.

"I wish some Person would come along," he said to himself. And just then he saw Skinkoots coming toward him.

Skinkoots had been eating a Bird-person, for there was a feather sticking to his nose.

"Say, you Skinkoots," said *Old*-man, "I am lonesome. Do not you suppose I ever want company?"

"Well, here I am," said Skinkoots. "What shall we do, you and I?"

"I am travelling, and I want some Person to go with me," said *Old*-man. "Come! That is what we will do. We will travel and see what is going on there."

"Where?" asked the Coyote, licking his chops, and spitting out the feather.

"Everywhere, of course," answered *Old*-man.

"All right," agreed Skinkoots. "If you know the way, lead on. I will follow." And so they

started travelling together in the forest, *Old*-man
ahead and Skinkoots behind. They got along
fine, because Skinkoots liked *Old*-man. He likes
all Old Persons and they are his friends.

Of course *Old*-man talked a good deal without
saying much that was worth while, and maybe
this made the Coyote careless of what came to
his ears. Anyhow, when the Sun was half-way
to his lodge in the West and they were in a deep
thicket of small fir-trees, *Old*-man said:

"Skinkoots, we shall soon come to a place
where we shall hear crying. It will come from
behind a large pine-tree up on that mountain
yonder. When you hear this crying, pass right
along as though you heard nothing. I know
who will be crying up there. It is a Bad-person
that cries only to make trouble. Do just as I
do. Hear nothing of this crying and pass
on."

Any Person could understand that. And
Skinkoots understood it, of course. But his
ears were already listening for the crying.

4

WHY SKINKOOTS'S ARMS ARE THIN

"Here we go up the mountain," said *Old*-man, as they came out of the thicket and commenced to climb. "This one is not so bad as some mountains I made, and on this one there are pine-trees at the top — large yellow pines that reach high."

When *Old*-man mentioned the pine-trees, Skinkoots thought more strongly of the "crying" that was up there, and he wondered and wondered what Person it was that cried. But he followed along behind, laughing a little at *Old*-man's clumsy climbing. Mountains were nothing to Skinkoots. But *Old*-man grew tired, and near the top he stopped to rest.

While he waited Skinkoots turned over a rotten log and caught a Mouse-person to eat. Just as he swallowed the Mouse-person he heard the crying and looked at *Old*-man to see if he, too, had caught the sound.

He could not tell, for *Old*-man was looking straight down the mountain and did not show that he had heard anything at all.

"Humph!" thought Skinkoots. "He must have heard it. Anybody could hear it, even the Fish-persons."

Just then the crying came again. But *Old*-man paid no attention to it, and began to climb the mountain as though nothing had happened — as though there were no crying at all.

Finally they came to the mountain's top, and here grew many, many large pine-trees with great tops that sang when the Winds blew. There was no underbrush to hide Persons here.

Beneath the great pines the ground was bare and only sunlight and shadows were on it. These danced whenever the Winds blew. They were dancing now. But Skinkoots did not notice this. He fixed his eyes on *Old*-man's back, and *Old*-man kept going on and on and on, as though he would never reach the place he was going to.

The Sun was nearly to his lodge in the West when suddenly the crying came again. It was

6

not loud crying, but it was pitiful, and full of suffering. Besides, it was a Baby that cried. Coyote knew this and trotted close to *Old*-man, to see what he was going to do about it. But *Old*-man was looking straight ahead as before. He did not even seem to travel any slower, and Skinkoots had mean thoughts of him then.

"His heart is a stone," he said to himself, listening to the crying. "Well, I cannot stand it to hear a Baby cry like that, if he *can*. I am not so very tender-hearted, either."

He stopped still to listen now. *Old*-man did not notice this, and was soon out of sight, believing that Skinkoots was following.

"Humph!" said Skinkoots. "I am going over there and see what is the matter with that poor Baby-person. I am not afraid of Babies, even if *Old*-man is."

"It is right over there by that big pine-tree — whatever it is that is crying. Here I go!"

Skinkoots is a fast traveller. He was soon beside the tree, but no Person was there! "This is funny," he said, walking around the tree. "I can hear the crying, and it is on this tree, too, but I do not see the one that cries."

He walked around the tree again and saw nothing at all. Four times he did this without seeing the Person that cried. "Oh, it is only some Person fooling me," he thought. And then, just as he was going to give it up and run on after *Old*-man, he saw it! It was right there on that pine-tree all the time, of course! It could not get away, for it was tied fast with ropes of bark; and it was a Baby-person.

"Poor Baby — poor Baby," said Skinkoots, going close to it. "Poor Baby — poor Baby!" But the Baby-person would not stop its crying, and Skinkoots stuck his fingers into the Baby-person's mouth.

Oh, ho! The crying stopped. Oh, ho! It stopped when Skinkoots stuck his fingers in the Baby-person's mouth! The Baby-person began to suck Coyote's fingers!

"Poor Baby — poor Baby," said Skinkoots,

8

letting it suck and suck until his hand was out of sight.

"Poor Baby — poor Baby," he said. And before he knew it his arm was being sucked in farther and farther, until his shoulder was against the Baby-person's lips.

"Say! I do not like this very well!" he said to himself, for the sucking was hurting him now.

"Something is going on here! I guess I have done enough, anyhow, and I will just take myself away from here before this Person cries again."

He pulled a little, but his arm would not come out. He pulled harder, and then even harder. Oh, ho! His arm did not move! He could not get it out of the mouth of the Baby-person. Oh, ho! Now he was afraid! Now he remembered what *Old*-man had told him. But *Old*-man was far away and still travelling.

"Hey, *Nu-laaaa-kin-nah! Nu-laaaa-kin-nah!*" he called, waking the Echo-person on the mountain with his shrill voice. "*Nu-laaaa-kin-nah,*

Nu-laaaa-kin-nah! Come and help me get my arm back."

By this time *Old*-man was almost to the end of the mountain. But Skinkoots's voice reaches far. *Old*-man heard it, and he stopped to listen.

"Oh, ho!" he said. "*Now* what is going on? I guess I know. That foolish Skinkoots-person is in trouble. That is what it is. And, oh, dear! I shall have to walk away back there, I suppose."

He began to grumble and find fault with Skinkoots, who kept calling: "Hey, *Nu-laaa-kin-nah, Nu-laaa-kin-nah!* Come and help me get my arm back!"

The Sun had gone into his lodge when at last *Old*-man got there. He could scarcely see, so dark was the mountain-top now.

"Where are you, Skinkoots?" he asked, when he was near.

"Here I am, *Nu-la-kin-nah*. This Bad-person will not let go of my arm. He is hurting me. Oh! Oh! Ouch! Hurry, *Nu-la-kin-nah!* Hurry!"

WHY SKINKOOTS'S ARMS ARE THIN

Old-man came close. "Oh, ho!" he said. "This is the Crying-person that holds you! Did not I tell you not to hear him cry? Did not I tell you that he only cried to make trouble? Did not I tell you to pass on? Say, didn't I?"

"Yes. Oh, yes, *Nu-la-kin-nah*. Yes, you did. But I thought I could stop this Person's crying. I only stuck my fingers in its mouth. That is all I did, and then ——"

"Yes, I know all about it," growled *Old*-man. "Now you stand to one side while I kill this Bad-person."

Skinkoots stepped to one side and *Old*-man struck the Crying-person with his war-club — Swow! And the Person died.

But it took a long time and much pulling to get Skinkoots's arm out of the Baby-person's mouth. At last it came out, though.

Oh, ho! It was sucked to shreds, and was thin! Only skin and muscle were left! Oh, ho!

"Oh, dear — look at my arm, *Nu-la-kin-*

nah!" whimpered Skinkoots. "Look!" And he held it up.

"Yes, I see it, and it serves you right, Skinkoots. Yes, it serves you just right.

"Oh, ho! Now your arm will stay like that. Yes, and all your children that are born from this day onward shall have arms like the one the Crying-person sucked. Oh, ho!"

The words that *Nu-la-kin-nah, Old*-man, spoke that day are true. And now you know why Skinkoots has such skinny arms.

Ho!

II

THE FROG AND THE ANTELOPE

THERE was a village on Tobacco Plains. Antelope was Chief there. He was the fastest runner. His Medicine was strong. No Person could beat him at running. Many had tried. All gave it up. Antelope was the fastest runner!

There was another village on Tobacco Plains. Frog was Chief there. He could not run fast. But he was a smart man.

One day when his People were playing games he said to them: "Listen! The Antelope is *faster* than I am. But I am *smarter* than he is. I will prove this to you. Stay where you are until I come back."

He hopped along the trail that led to the Antelope village. When he found the Chief's lodge he went inside. They smoked the pipe there, and then the Antelope Chief began to brag about his running. "No Person can beat me," he said. "I can just trot along and beat most Persons."

"I like racing, myself," said the Frog Chief, passing the pipe to Antelope. "All my People like racing."

"But you cannot run — ha-ha-ha!" laughed the Antelope, taking a long draw on the pipe.

"Oh, I don't know about that. I am not so slow at running and I am a fast thinker," said the Frog Chief.

"Of course you would not say that you would race with *me*, though," smiled the Antelope, handing back the pipe.

"I might," said the Frog Chief slowly.

"What is that?" asked the Antelope. "You *might?*"

"Yes."

"When?"

"To-morrow."

"Where?"

14

THE FROG AND THE ANTELOPE

"Here; along the trail between our villages. I cannot run well where the ground is rough, you know. I must have a smooth place."

"Ha-ha-ha!" laughed the Antelope. "How far shall we run?"

"From your village to mine and back again," answered the Frog seriously.

"All right," agreed the Antelope. "I suppose I shall be laughed at for racing with *you*. But I will race just the same. A Person must use his power or he will lose it."

"Yes," said the Frog Chief, scratching his nose. "I am sure you will be laughed at, all right. Now, what will you bet on our race?"

"Bet? Why, anything — everything I have. What have you got to bet?"

"Well, not much," sighed the Frog Chief. "But you will admit that our clothes are pretty. I will bet my clothes, and all my tribe will do the same. How will that suit you?"

"Fine!" smiled the Antelope. "I like nice clothes."

The Frog's clothes were green and beautiful. Besides, they were always cool in summer.

"Fine! Be here at sunrise," smiled the Antelope, thinking of all the nice clothes that would be his after the race.

"I will be here," promised the Frog Chief, "and I will bring my whole tribe. Ho!"

Then he went out, and down the trail to his village, *hopping, hopping, hopping,* and *thinking, thinking, thinking,* till he got home to his lodge.

When he was gone the Antelope made his People a speech. He told them to go to a side-hill at sunrise to watch the race. "When it is finished," he said, "I shall have more clothes than I need. I will divide them among you, and you know that the Frog-person's clothes are fine in summer. I suppose I shall be laughed at for racing this Person," he added, smiling, "but think of the pretty clothes we shall have to pay for the laughing. Be on the hillside at sunrise. I have spoken." Then he went back to his lodge to laugh.

THE FROG AND THE ANTELOPE

The Frog Chief did not make a speech to his tribe. He just went quietly into his lodge and kept *thinking* and *smoking* and *thinking* till morning was near. *Then* he went outside and called his People.

"Follow me!" he said, and began hopping up the trail toward the Antelope's village. All his People were behind him, *hopping, hopping, hopping* along, *wondering* and *wondering* and *wondering* what was going on in their Chief's head. But nobody asked him. They just hopped along, each one tending to his own business of *hopping* until they were all there.

The Sun was not yet up, and the air was fine and clear. "Now listen to me, all of you," said the Frog Chief, looking back along the trail that was green with Frog-persons. "I am going to run a race with the Antelope Chief this morning at sunrise. I have bet all my clothes and yours on it. If I lose this race we shall have bad times. That is all."

The Frogs laid their hands upon their mouths, for they were astonished.

"There must be no mistakes made here this morning," went on the Frog Chief sternly. "Pay attention to me!

"First Frog, turn around! Now, you hop one long hop down this trail. That is it. Now hide yourself and stay still.

"Second Frog, turn around! Now *you* hop one long hop past the first Frog. That is it! Now, hide yourself, and stay still.

"Third Frog, turn around! Now, *you* hop one long hop past the second Frog. That is it! Now hide yourself, and stay still."

He made enough Frogs turn around and hop one long hop past the last one until they reached to his village along the trail. And when the last one hopped into his place near their village, not one of them could be seen. But there were Frogs all the way from the Antelope's village to the Frog's village. And they were just one long hop apart.

"Now, you Trail-frogs, listen!" said the Frog Chief. "You are *all* in this race; every one of you, and there must be no mistakes made if you want to save your clothes. When we start this race, I will hop one long hop down the trail, then number one will hop one long hop down the trail, then number two, and number three, and number four, and so on clear to our own village, each one stopping right where he lands after hopping one long hop. But the hopper must hop just ahead of this fast Antelope-person. Understand what I am doing? I am cheating him. We all look alike! He will think the last hopper down there by our village is *me*.

"Now listen again! As soon as you hop and land, turn around. Then when the Antelope starts back, you will be ready to beat him back by hopping one long hop just as you did before, only you must hop the other way. If anybody does not understand this smartness he had better say so now. There must be no mistakes here this morning, if we want to save our clothes."

Nobody said a word. "All right," said the

19

Frog Chief. "The rest of you come along with me."

"Good morning," bowed the Antelope, stretching himself, and looking toward the East, where the Sun was coming. "Good morning. You have brought many People with you," he smiled.

"Yes, quite a few. More than you realize, I think. We are not very tall, you know," answered the Frog Chief.

"Are you ready?" asked the Antelope, bounding about to show off.

"Yes, I am all ready," said the Frog Chief, "and the Sun is rising, too."

"All right, then." The Antelope Chief whistled, and out of their lodges came all his People. They ran up on the hillside and stood still to watch the race.

"Here we go," laughed the Antelope Chief, trotting down the trail. But the Frog-person was always a little ahead of him.

"Well! He is faster than I thought," said the

Antelope, beginning to *run*. Still the Frog was a little ahead of him — always a little *ahead*.

"Well! This Person is not so *slow!*" he thought, and began to go like the wind.

But always the Frog-person was a little ahead of him — one long hop ahead.

He began to think of his property now. Oh, ho! The Frog-person was a little ahead when finally he reached the Frog village, and turned to race back.

"I will beat him now," he thought. "This way is up-hill." He ran as fast as he could go, pounding the trail with his hoofs. But, as before, always the Frog-person hopped a little ahead of him, till, out of breath, he fell down near his own lodge — beaten!

Oh, ho! Now everybody began to *laugh*. They laughed very hard, and while they were laughing the Frog Chief hopped near the Antelope, whose sides were panting so fast he could not speak. Oh, ho!

"A little running seems to *tire* you," smiled

the Frog Chief, looking around at all the property he had won in the race. His sides were not panting. He had only hopped two long hops — *one* down the trail and *one* up again.

"I guess you are a Short-of-breath-person," he added, sitting down.

"Well, you have beaten me, and I admit it," panted the Antelope Chief. "You are a very fast runner. That is all I can say. I misjudged you. But I *know* now."

"Oh, I am not so very fast at *running*," replied the Frog Chief, beginning to gather up the Antelope's property, "but I spend a good deal of time *thinking*. I am a pretty fast *thinker*, you will find."

Ho!

III

CO–PEE

THE fire had burned so low that only coals glowed in the ashes. Walks-in-the-water, who had listened with the children to the story of "The Frog and the Antelope," put some birch-bark on the red coals, and instantly the bark caught fire, making the lodge bright again.

"Whooo-whooo-hoo-hoo," came from the forest back of the white lodge.

"*Co*-pee," whispered the children, their eyes wide and their faces serious.

"Ahh — *Co*-pee," smiled Two-comes-over-the-hill, listening. His gray head turned expectantly and his old eyes grew merry.

"Whooo-whooo-hoo-hoo." A Horned-owl, as though to oblige the aged Medicine-man and his company, hooted again. His voice, deep and clear in the keen air, sounded very close.

23

"*Co*-pee," whispered Two-comes-over-the-hill. "He is a different Person now. But when the world was young as you are, *Co*-pee was a wicked Person. Our People remember when *Co*-pee was bad, and even to-day, when children cry for nothing at all, their mothers frighten them to silence by saying: 'Hush! *Co*-pee is near. He will come and get you.'"

He smiled thoughtfully, and the children looked at each other with sudden understanding. "But *Co*-pee is not a Bad-person to-day, even if the *Upsmuckkinick* (Blackfeet and others) *are* afraid of him. No, *Co*-pee is now a Good-person, and I will tell you how he learned to be good.

"It was *Old*-man, of course, that changed *Co*-pee's cold heart and made it warm, but this was no easy thing to do, as you shall see.

"Rain was falling. The forests were dark, even in the daytime. And now it was night. Oh, ho! Now it was night! Everywhere the world was wet, even beneath the spruce-trees, where most always the ground is dry. Every

Person stayed in his lodge and was glad he had a lodge to stay in, too.

"But in all the lodges there were only twelve children. The bad weather had made the children cross, and *Co*-pee, hearing them crying, had come in the night and taken them away one by one until there were only twelve left. Nobody knew what he had done with them. He could not have eaten all, but even when the day came and mothers looked until their eyes ached, no children came back.

"Oh, ho! What could the mothers do? Nothing! Nothing at all, besides trying to keep their children from crying. Whenever one of the twelve children would cry at night, every Old Woman would say: 'Hush! Hush! *Co*-pee will get you.'

"This was all they could do. Every Person watched the children at night to keep them from crying. And every night, when the darkness spread over the forests, *Co*-pee hung around the lodges where the twelve children lived.

Often the mothers heard his voice and trembled. Often he called as he did to-night, and quick as a flash out went every fire in the lodges. But putting out the fires did no good at all. *Co*-pee sees best when the world is dark.

"Finally, every Person that had a child — and some that had none at all — went to *Old*-man's lodge and told him about all that was going on.

"'We are getting old, some of us,' said the Chipmunk-person, 'and if that *Co*-pee-person keeps on taking our children — well, the first thing *you* know you will be living alone on this world, that is all.'

"'What is this — what is this?' asked *Old*-man, lighting his Medicine-pipe. 'What is all this?'

"'It is this,' said the Chipmunk-person; 'unless you do something to *Co*-pee most of us here will die and leave no children behind us. I have only two left, and my Woman and I are getting old. Besides, it is the same with a lot of other Persons. The Mouse-person has only two children left, the Pine-squirrel has none at all, the Rabbit and his Woman one, the Grouse told me to-day her last is gone; and look how old *she* is. Over on that hill by the lake of the Duck-persons Old Man Mole and his Woman are starving their two children because they dare not leave their lodge to get food for them. And besides all this, who ate the Mud-hen's child yesterday right before her eyes?'

"'Whooo-whooo-hoo-hoo!'

"Oh, ho! *Co*-pee was on *Old*-man's lodge-poles! Oh, ho! He had heard every word!

"The Chipmunk-person ran under *Old*-man's legs, and everybody hid. There was no talking now, I can tell you! All was quiet in *Old*-man's lodge. Only the rain outside made a noise. Oh, ho!

"'Whooo-whooo-hoo-hoo!' called *Co*-pee again.

"'*You!* That is who!' cried the Chipmunk from under *Old*-man's legs. But his voice trembled frightfully.

"'Go away from here, *Co*-pee,' called *Old*-man. 'I have company.'

"'Oh, I *know* you have,' said *Co*-pee. 'And some of your company better look out, too. You know whom I mean, I guess.'

"'Well, you go away from this lodge! Do you hear me? Clear away — a long way away!' said *Old*-man. And, of course, *Co*-pee had to do that.

"'Oh, all right,' he said, 'but some of your company had better hide.'

"'I believe I *will* have to do something to that *Co*-pee-person,' said *Old*-man, thoughtfully, when *Co*-pee had gone.

"'And, say, you Chipmunk, take care of yourself,' he advised, when his visitors were ready to go home to their own lodges.

"'I will do the best I can; you may depend on that. But if you do not see me to-morrow, you will know what happened,' snapped the Chipmunk, for he was getting scared again, and pretended he was angry to cover his fright.

"'Please do not wait, *Old*-man,' begged the Grouse-person. 'What the Chipmunk has told is true. My! I would not be in that Chipmunk-person's place for anything! Well, good night,' she said, 'and say,' she added, lingering behind the others a little, 'please do not repeat what that Chipmunk-person said about my age. I am not so old.'

"'I think we had better travel alone, don't you?' asked the Mouse-person when they were all outside.

"'Oh, I suppose so,' smiled the Chipmunk. 'I am not so popular as I was. Good night, all.'

"It was darker than ever in the forest, after being so long in *Old*-man's lodge beside the fire. But the Chipmunk-person ran across the little open space by *Old*-man's lodge, and was gone in a flash.

"He ran fast, with his tail up, scooting between the big trees, ready every minute to climb if *Co*-pee came after him, without seeing a single

29

Person until he came to a patch of kinnikinic-berries. He ran right onto them before he saw them, of course.

"Chipmunk was hungry and the berries were red. 'I will eat a few, anyhow,' he said. 'I don't think *Co*-pee is near this place.'

"He sat up on his haunches, with a fat red berry in his hands, and just as he took the first bite — Swow! *Co*-pee struck at him — Swow! But he missed! Oh, ho! He missed!

"Like a flash Chipmunk was up a tree and safely hidden behind a big limb.

"*Co*-pee could not climb, and flying would not help him with Chipmunk safe in the tree, so he grew cunning.

"'Say, you!' he called, 'your father wants you to come home. I promised I would find you and tell you this.'

"'I have n't any father. He is dead,' laughed the Chipmunk.

"'I mean your *mother* wants you,' lied *Co*-pee.

"'I *have n't* any mother. You ate her last

summer,' laughed the Chipmunk, moving out a little so he could see his enemy.

"'Well, I guess it was your *grandmother*, then,' said *Co*-pee. 'I noticed she was old, anyhow. Whoever it was said to tell you to bring her some of these berries; and I have told you.'

"'Oh, she did, did she?' mocked the Chipmunk. But he *did* have a grandmother, you see, and she *was* old, and he loved her dearly. His grandmother was the Frog-person and she lived with him and his Woman. 'Maybe grandmother wants me,' he thought. 'I had better go home, if I can get there.'

"'Say, you *Co*-pee-person, I will go home now, if you will let me.'

"'Who is stopping you, I should like to know?' laughed *Co*-pee, stepping back from the tree, to fool the Chipmunk.

"'Well, if you will just shut your big eyes, I will try it — that is, I will come down,' said the Chipmunk, crawling out on the limb.

"'They *are* shut already,' said *Co*-pee, covering his eyes with both his hands. Only he spread his fingers! Oh, ho! He spread his fingers and looked between them!

"Down the tree ran the Chipmunk, never thinking that *Co*-pee could see with his hands over his eyes. Down — down he came till just when he touched the ground Old *Co*-pee *snatched* at him! Oh, ho! He missed! He missed! But not altogether, for *Co*-pee's talons scratched the Chipmunk's back. Oh, ho! He scratched his back lengthwise!

"The scratches never went away. They are there to this day. All the Chipmunks wear them. And now you know why their backs are scratched.

"But even now after Chipmunk got away *Co*-pee followed fast, striking and clawing until Chipmunk came to a hollow log and popped in.

"'Ha-ha-ha!' he laughed. 'You never touched me,' he lied. 'Why don't you come in out of the rain, *Co*-pee?'

"'Oh, I will wait here,' growled *Co*-pee. 'You will come out some time.'

"'Of course I will, but you will be gone. *Old-man* will take care of you. He is going to do something to *you*. He *said* so, and every Person will be glad. Nobody likes you, not even the Skunk-person, and goodness knows he is mean enough. He is almost as mean as you are.'

"Nobody answered. All was quiet outside the log. Chipmunk could hear the rain pattering on it. His back hurt him, but he felt pretty proud.

"'I will see if he is gone, I guess,' he said to himself, thinking of his old grandmother, the Frog-person. He stuck his nose out of the hole just a little and listened. Nothing but the rain made a noise. 'I guess he is gone,' he whispered to himself, poking his head out. 'Yep — *Co*-pee is *gone*. Ha-ha! Well, here I go,' he said. And in no time at all he was home in his own lodge.

"'What is the matter with your back?' asked

33

his grandmother, the Frog-person, when Chipmunk sat down by the fire there.

"'*Co*-pee scratched me, Grandmother,' said Chipmunk.

"'Is it sore?' she asked, hopping near him.

"'Some,' said Chipmunk soberly.

"'Well, I will fix it,' she said, tossing him into a skin-kettle where there was soup and much tallow-fat.

"The tallow-fat stuck to some of the bad scratches, and that is why some of the marks on the Chipmunk's back are nearly white, even to-day.

"Of course the Chipmunk was all wet with the soup when his grandmother lifted him out of the skin-kettle, and he began at once to wash his face, for he is a very neat Person.

"'You will see something pretty soon now,' he said knowingly, his thoughts on the wicked *Co*-pee. '*Old*-man is going to do something to that Person, and it may happen any time now.'

34

"'Hark!' said his grandmother, the Frog-person, going to the door of their lodge. 'A child is crying! *Co*-pee will take it! Oh, dear, oh, dear! And there are so few left. Hark!'

"'Why! I do believe the crying is in this lodge! Who can it be? See! *Your* children are laughing, not crying. Oh, look! Grandchild! One is crying. But it is some other Person's child that cries. Move it near the door! Move it quick! If *Co*-pee comes he may take one of *yours* instead of the crying child!'

"Chipmunk moved the crying child near the lodge door. 'Hush! Hush!' he said soothingly. '*Co*-pee will get you.'

"Oh, ho! Just then a feathered arm with long, sharp fingers reached inside and, Swow! the child was gone!

"Oh, ho! There was nothing at all where the child had been. *Co*-pee had come and carried it away. Oh, ho!

"'Whose child *was* that?' asked the Chipmunk, putting some wood on his fire.

"'I do not know,' said his Woman. 'I never saw it before.'

"'Nor I,' said his grandmother, the Frog-person. 'I did not even see it come here.'

"'Well, I guess I will go and find out,' said the Chipmunk. 'It was *some* Person's child.'

"He was gone until morning. He had visited every lodge he could find, but no Person had lost a child that night, not one.

"'Whose *was* it?' asked his Wife anxiously, as Chipmunk sat down by the fire.

"'Nobody's,' said Chipmunk, warming his hands.

"'Is your back hurting you, Grandchild?' asked his grandmother, the Frog-person, thinking perhaps his head was wrong.

"'My back is all right, Grandmother. But there is something going on here. That was *nobody's* child,' said the Chipmunk, looking foolish.

"His grandmother, the Frog-person, gave him some soup, and his Woman spread a robe over his shoulders. Then they both sat down across the fire and looked at Chipmunk, their hands over their mouths. They were astonished, and by this sign they said so without words.

"By this time *Co*-pee had carried the crying child to his lodge. No Person knows where it was, but we know it was across the mountains. When *Co*-pee got there he put the child inside with more than a hundred other children, and then he went after dry wood.

"There was a bright fire in the lodge and the crying child began to laugh.

"'Oh, there is nothing to laugh at here,' said a child of the Pine-squirrel-person. 'He may eat any of us to-morrow, or even to-night. You better not laugh. Remember your mother is sad to-night.'

"'My mother sad?' laughed the crying child. 'I have no mother. I have no father. I never had a mother! I never had a father! Nobody is sad about me. Listen! Gather around me, you children! I am no crying child. I am *Old-*

man! Ha-ha-ha! I am going to do something
to this *Co*-pee-person. Now listen!

"'When he comes back we must all be dancing
as though our hearts were glad. Where is his
drum? Oh, I see it. It is a good one, too — a
fine one! Here we go! Around the fire, all of
you!

"'Tu-tum-tu-tum!' *Old*-man, for it was he,
began beating *Co*-pee's drum, and all the children began to dance.

"'Nobody must stop until I say so,' said *Old*-
man. And now he began to sing:

> " ' *Co-pee likes us,*
> *Co-pee likes us,*
> *Co-pee likes us,*
> *Co*-pee likes us.'

"*Co*-pee heard the drum and the singing and
ran back to his lodge to see what was going on.

"'Oh, ho! This is fine!' he laughed. 'Have
a good time, children — have a good time!'

> " ' *Co-pee likes us,*
> *Co-pee likes us,*

38

CO–PEE

Co-pee likes us,
Co-pee likes us,'

sang *Old*-man, all the time beating the drum, 'tu-tum-tu-tum,' till *Co*-pee joined the circle and began to dance with the children.

"Oh, ho! This was what *Old*-man expected, and when *Co*-pee came dancing around the fire with his back to *Old*-man — Swow! he struck him dead with his war-club. Oh, ho! *Co*-pee lay dead by the fire in his own lodge.

"*Old*-man, who had changed himself into a baby to help the stolen children, now changed back again, and was himself. He bent over *Co*-pee and touched his big eyes. Pop! They burst! and out flew two little Owls, blinking at the firelight.

"'Say, you,' said *Old*-man to the two small Owls, 'go and make your living as others do. Never trouble your neighbors! Never steal children! Just tend to your own business, or I will do something to *you!*'

"The two young Owls flew away, and had

many children.   None have been wicked.   None
will ever bother People.   And you know why.

"As soon as the young Owls were gone, *Old*-
man started back across the mountains with all
the stolen children.   He brought each safely to
its own mother.   Then everybody was happy
and nobody was afraid of *Co*-pee, because he was
dead.

"Ho!"

IV

COYOTE AND *OLD*–MAN'S EYES

THE Winds were sleeping. The tall grasses stood still, as though they were waiting. Even the leaves on the trees were resting because the Winds were asleep. The Sun was in the Middle of the Sky, so that the Shadow of Skinkoots was under his belly as he travelled. He was beside a great River that talked loud as it went along, because the Winds were sleeping.

"Ha-ha-ha." Some Person was laughing.

Skinkoots stopped and looked around. Now he heard nothing but the River's talking. "I thought I heard laughing," he said to himself. "My ears fooled me, I guess."

He was following a Deer trail along the River. "Ha-ha-ha." Skinkoots heard that laughing again. He stopped and looked all around. Then he saw a Person acting queerly.

"Something is going on here," he said. "I guess I will go and see what that Person is doing over there."

He trotted over that way and then he saw *Old*-man under a Birch-tree.

Skinkoots sat down and watched him. But he did not speak. He only watched to see what was going on there. *Old*-man was shaking the Birch-tree, and his head was bent backward. When *Old*-man shook the Tree, Skinkoots saw something drop on *Old*-man's face. But he could not tell what it was that fell.

Whatever it was it made *Old*-man glad, and he laughed "Ha-ha-ha!" when the thing fell on his face.

"What is going on here, I wonder," thought Skinkoots, going closer. "I will see about this."

Just then *Old*-man took out his eyes and tossed them up into the Birch-tree's top. Then he bent his head backward and shook the Tree. Oh, ho! His eyes came back! They fell into their holes in his face!

42

"He is a Smart Person," thought Skinkoots. "But if he does that thing again I will fix him. I will steal his eyes."

Just then *Old*-man took out his eyes again and tossed them into the top of the Birch-tree. Then he bent his head far backward and shook the Tree.

The eyes started to fall down again, of course, but Skinkoots saw the eyes coming back. He jumped over *Old*-man's head and grabbed them. Oh, ho! Skinkoots caught *Old*-man's eyes while they were falling.

So softly he jumped *Old*-man did not know Skinkoots was around there. But his eyes did not come back. Skinkoots had them.

Old-man shook the Tree hard, and waited with his head bent far backward. His eyes did not come back.

"I guess my eyes are on the Ground," he said, and Skinkoots heard him. *Old*-man staggered around, feeling for his eyes. His head struck the Birch-tree and many trees, besides. But

43

he could not find his eyes.   Skinkoots had them.

Old-man kept going farther and farther away from the Birch-tree, looking for his eyes and talking to himself.   Skinkoots followed along, laughing inside, until he heard *Old*-man crying: "Oh, my eyes are lost — my eyes are lost."

Then Skinkoots was a little sorry.   But he said: "I am going to have some fun with *Old*-man while his eyes are gone."

He was talking to himself, of course, because nobody else was around there.   He ran around *Old*-man and got ahead of him.   "I will sit down and when he comes along I will poke my fingers in his eye-holes," he laughed.   "I will have some fun with the Blind-person."

But just then *Old*-man knew what was going on there.   His Medicine had told him.   He came creeping along, bumping things, till he reached Skinkoots.   And then Skinkoots stuck his fingers into *Old*-man's empty eye-sockets.

"Ouch!   What is this?" cried *Old*-man.   But he knew well enough.   And he grabbed Skinkoots!   Oh, ho!   He grabbed him!

"Now I will fix you for stealing my eyes," said *Old*-man. And he took out Skinkoots's eyes; and, besides, he put his own eyes into his own face!

Oh, ho! Now Skinkoots could not see. Now he ran into things, and *Old*-man laughed. "Ha-ha! Now it is your turn!" he cried from far off, because he had gone away from there with Skinkoots's eyes.

Skinkoots did not cry. But he was having a hard time, bumping things around there. "I know what I will do," he said; "I will find two good Huckleberries. That is what I want now — two good Huckleberries."

He asked every bush he struck, "What are you, Bush?" till at last one said: "Why, I am a Huckleberry-bush, of course."

"Well, you are the one I am looking for," said Skinkoots. And he picked two Huckleberries and poked them into his head where his eyes had been.

But these two Huckleberries were not very good ones, and he began looking for better ones.

45

He could see now, but not very well. He travelled far, and then he heard a Boy-person call: "Sister, come over this way! Here are some good Huckleberries!"

"That is just what I am looking for," said Skinkoots to himself.

He ran over there and shot that Boy-person, took off his Robe, and put it on himself. "Now I look all right, I guess," he said. And just then he heard the girl calling for her brother.

"Where are you, Brother?" she called. "Where are those good Huckleberries?"

"Over here," answered Skinkoots. "Right over here, Sister."

He had moved a little, so she would not see her dead brother, and when she came he said: "What was going on last night where we came from?"

"Oh, you know what was going on as well as I do," answered the Girl-person, thinking Skinkoots was her brother. "We danced with the Old Woman who has Skinkoots's eyes."

When she said that he killed her, and took off her Robe and put it on himself. "Now I look all right, I guess. I will go and find that Old Woman who has my eyes." And in no time at all he was there.

The Old Woman was a Frog-person, and she thought Skinkoots was that Girl, of course, because he wore her Robe.

Skinkoots went right into the Old Woman's lodge and said: "Now I have got you! Now I will fix you for dancing with my eyes!"

He did not even ask the Old Woman where she got his eyes. He killed her with his arrows. Then he took her Robe off and put it on himself. "Now I look all right, I guess," he said. "I will go to that Dance myself."

In no time at all he was there where that Dance was going on. It was dark in there and he danced.

Everybody thought he was the Old Frog-woman who had his eyes, and they all danced, and they all sang, except Skinkoots.

The fire in there where that Dance was going on was always growing dimmer and dimmer. At last it went out! Oh, ho! The fire went out. Now it was very dark in there.

Just then all the Persons in there heard a strange voice. It sang:

"*I am going to dance for Skinkoots's eyes,*
I am going to dance for Skinkoots's eyes,
I am going to dance for Skinkoots's eyes,
I am going to dance for Skinkoots's eyes."

It was Skinkoots, of course, who sang that song. He was dancing in the dark, and when he came to the lodge door, he jumped out! Oh, ho! He was gone, and right in the doorway the others found the Old Frog-woman's Robe.

Then Everybody knew that the Old Woman was dead and that Skinkoots had been there.

Ho!

V

COYOTE AND GRIZZLY BEAR

ONE day in the Springtime the Grizzly Bear-person was digging roots on a hillside. He was very busy because he was hungry, and he noticed nothing around him. He was not afraid of other Persons, and therefore did not have to be on guard all the time.

While he dug the roots little rocks would roll down the hillside. They made a noise, of course, striking against the trees and bushes below him, but he did not care. He was not afraid.

Skinkoots was trotting along in the forest looking for meat when he heard a rock strike a tree not far away.

"Oh, ho!" he said. "Now what is going on, I wonder? I will go and see who it is that is throwing these stones that may strike Persons."

He trotted along till he could see the hillside where the Grizzly Bear was digging roots.

"Oh! It is that big lump of a Person, is it? Well, I will play with him awhile, I guess. I have nothing else to do."

In no time at all he climbed the hill and found a hiding-place above the Grizzly Bear-person, who never looked up from his root-digging.

Skinkoots watched him a long time. Then he stuck his head out and called: "Hey, you small-eyed big Person. You are homely!"

The Grizzly Bear stopped digging roots and looked all around, but saw nobody at all. He thought he was mistaken, and began to dig more roots.

"Hey, you Left-handed-one," called Skinkoots. "Your tail makes me laugh. Ha-ha-ha-ha-ha-ha!"

He laughed too long. Oh, ho! he laughed too long. Grizzly Bear saw him!

Up the hill he went after Skinkoots, who began to run around a great rock, with the Grizzly

Bear-person after him. Round and round they went, so fast they looked like one Person, till Skinkoots stubbed his toe.

Oh, ho! He staggered. Then he fell over a cliff. Swow!

The fall dazed him. He felt something in his hands. He closed them. Then he looked to see what he held in his hands. They were Buffalo horns. He had fallen upon the skull of a Buffalo Bull.

He stood up. The horns stuck to his hands! He could not let them go! He stepped on one and was pulling, when he heard the Grizzly Bear-person coming through the brush, near a river.

"I guess I do not want these horns to leave my hands yet," he said. "I need them."

On came the Grizzly Bear. When he was in plain sight Skinkoots made a noise like a Buffalo Bull and charged him. Oh, ho! He stabbed the Bear with the horns while he made the noise of a Buffalo-person.

The horns hurt the Grizzly Bear, and, besides, he thought the Person who was fighting him was a Buffalo Bull. He turned and ran away. Oh, ho! He jumped into the river and crossed it. Skinkoots had whipped the Grizzly Bear-person! Ho!

VI

BOY AND HIS WIFE

ONCE there was an Old Woman. She had only one son, and she and this Boy lived in a lodge together.

One day when they were sitting there the Old Woman said: "Son, I am growing old. You are big enough to have a Woman of your own. Go up that hill yonder, and look around."

The Boy went out and climbed the hill. Then he looked around. Far off he saw many smokes. The smokes looked very far off.

"A village is there," he said to himself. "I will go that way, for I must find a Woman for my lodge. My mother is growing old."

When he got to the village the People were playing with a ball. The ball was made of Deerskin stuffed with Deer's hair, and the People kicked it around and laughed to see it roll.

"Where is the Chief's lodge?" the Boy asked the first Person he met.

The Person pointed, and the Boy saw a fine lodge in the centre of the village. It was painted in many colors, and was taller than the rest. He went to this lodge and entered. A Crow was sitting near the fire smoking his pipe.

"How!" said the Boy politely, but looking around a little.

"How! How!" said the Crow. "Why do you come here? What do you want?"

"I am looking for a Woman," answered the Boy. "My mother is getting old."

"Oh, that is it, is it?" said the Crow, passing him the pipe. "Well, I have two daughters. You may have one of them. There they are, over there."

The Boy took the pipe. Then he looked and saw two young Women sitting on a robe. They were exactly alike, and both were handsome.

BOY AND HIS WIFE

"Which do you think is the younger?" asked the Crow, stirring his fire.

"That one." The Boy pointed.

"Yes, you are right," said the Crow, "and you may have her. But I must tell you one thing first. Do not let her work out-of-doors. Keep her in your lodge. Let her cook your food and make your clothes. If you always do this you will have no trouble. But if you forget and let her work outside — well, don't you do it — that is all."

The Boy's mother was glad when he brought the young Woman to her lodge. "I will help her," she said. And she *did* help her.

"Now you will have to chop and bring in the wood," said the Boy's mother. "I am growing too old."

The Boy always chopped and brought in the wood so that his wife could work always inside the lodge.

One day when he was chopping the wood he grew thirsty. "I will go to the lodge," he thought, "and get a drink of water." But there was no water in the kettle — none at all. The kettle was empty.

"I will bring some water," said his young wife, getting up.

"No, I will get the water myself," said the Boy, reaching for the kettle.

"Oh, let your wife bring the water, Son," said his mother. "It will not hurt her to fetch water once."

Before the Boy knew what was going on, his young wife took the kettle and went out of the lodge.

"I guess this will be all right," thought the Boy, and he sat down to wait for his wife to bring the water. He waited and waited, but she did not come back. Oh, ho! She did not bring the water!

"Now we have done it," said the Boy. "Night has come and my wife has not brought the water. I let her work outside. Now what shall I do?"

"Well, sleep," said his mother. "In the morning perhaps you will know what to do about it."

The Boy slept and he dreamed. When morning came he got up and went out of the lodge. He went up on that hill and looked around. The smokes were still there, so he went again to the Crow's lodge, and told him what had happened.

"Well," said the Crow Chief when he had listened. "This is about what I expected. But you are a good Boy. Take my other daughter. She is better than the other, anyhow."

"No," replied the Boy. "I want my own Woman. I will hunt for her. If I do not find her, I will come back here and get this one."

He travelled back to his mother's lodge. "Cook food for me," he told her. "I shall be gone a long time. If you hear Thunder three times do not look for me. I shall be dead."

Then he cut a Fox-skin into strips and wound his body with the fur.

Far from his mother's lodge he began to call: "Oh, Medicine-persons, help me find my Woman — oh, Medicine-persons, help me find my Woman!"

Oh, ho! These Persons began to come to him. They sat in council with him in the forest, and they smoked together. Finally the oldest Thunder-bird stood up and asked: "What is it that you want of us, Brother?"

The Boy said: "I am sorry, but I have lost my Woman. I want you to help me find her."

"Well," said the oldest Thunder-bird, "of course we know where she is. But she is in a very Bad Place, I can tell you *that*."

"Can I go there?" asked the Boy, ready to start.

"Yes, and we will go with you. But you must be very careful. Come, before the Sun goes to his lodge," said one of the Persons.

The Boy followed the three Thunder-birds out of the forest, and on up into the high mountains where the snows live forever. They were on the top of a very high mountain when they came to a large, Flat Rock. The Wind was howling and little snows were dancing on it.

"This is the place," said the oldest Thunderbird. "Now, you go and lift up that Rock and look. You will see a deep hole beneath it; and another thing, besides."

The Boy bent his head so the dancing snows would not stab his face, and lifted the Rock.

Oh, ho! There was a Big Rattlesnake in the hole, and the Boy stepped back.

"What is it that you want here?" asked the Big Rattlesnake, coiled to strike.

"I want my Woman back," said the Boy, remembering that he had strong Helpers.

"Hey, you, down there!" called the Big Rattlesnake to Persons down deep in the hole "Here is the Boy after his wife!"

"Well, he cannot have her. Send him away," came a deep voice from down in the dark hole.

Just then the Big Rattlesnake saw the three

Thunder-birds, and he was afraid. "We had better let him have her, I think," he said, uncoiling and moving back a little.

"No-oo-oo-oo!" came up out of the deep hole. "No-no-no!"

Oh, ho! Now the Boy knew his wife was there. But what could he do about it?

He went back to where the Thunder-birds waited, and told them just what he had seen and heard.

"Of course!" said the oldest Thunder-bird. "We will smoke now. Sit down, Brother, and maybe something will happen here."

He lit the Medicine-pipe. Oh, ho! Then he was gone! He was not there! Where there were *four*, there were now only *three!*

Then the Boy saw a black cloud, and heard Thunder — once!

Swow! The oldest Thunder-bird struck the Rock with fire. The mountain trembled. But the big Flat Rock did not break.

Oh, ho! Now again there were *four* on the

The boy bent his head so the dancing snows would not stab his face,
and lifted the Rock

ground. Oldest Thunder-bird had returned, and at once lit the Medicine-pipe. He passed it to his Brother, next oldest Thunder-bird. Oh, ho! When this Person took the pipe he was gone! There were only *three* on the ground vhere there had been *four* Persons.

The Boy saw a black cloud over the big Flat Fock. He heard Thunder again. That was twice!

Swow! Second oldest Thunder-bird struck the big Flat Rock with fire that was blinding. But the Rock did not break.

Oh, ho! Now once more there were four Persons on the ground. Second oldest Thunder-bird had come back.

Quickly he lit the Medicine-pipe and passed it to his Brother, the youngest Thunder-bird. Oh, ho! As soon as his hands had taken it, youngest Thunder-bird was gone, and there were only three left on the ground.

A great black cloud covered the sky; Winds howled louder, and hail came like arrows from

61

the sky. The Boy heard *awful* Thunder. That
was three times.

Swow! The youngest Thunder-bird struck
the big Flat Rock with fire that crackled like
handfuls of small stones falling on hard things.

Swow! The world trembled and smelled of
burning things.

Then the Boy looked. The big Flat Rock was
smashed into little pieces. The whole mountain
was changed and slide-rock was where cliffs had
been. He saw snakes scattered as far as he
could see. But they were all *small*, and this is
why snakes never again dared to go above the
timber-line on a mountain!

The Boy ran to the big hole with fear in his
heart. And there was his Woman, safe and un-
harmed!

He raced back to thank the Thunder-birds,
but of course they were gone.

"Well, we will go to my mother's lodge now,"
said the Boy, taking his wife by the hand, "and
after this you must not work outside."

But when they got there the Old Woman was dead. She had heard it thunder *three times,* and thought her son was killed. So she died herself.

Ho!

VII

DEER–PERSONS

"LISTEN! Long ago the Deer-persons were bad. Everybody was afraid of them except the Mountain-lion and the Wolf-person. Even these had trouble with them.

"Of course the Mountain-lion-person had the best of it, for he springs upon their backs, and he is a heavy Person. His claws are sharp and his teeth are like those of the Wolf-person. But everybody was afraid of the Deer's teeth, for he had many, and both jaws were full of them in those days.

"You have seen the teeth of the Deer. You know that he has *no front teeth on his upper jaw*, and that there is only empty space all the way to the teeth far back. Besides this, you know that the Deer has a *few front teeth on his lower jaw*, edged like knives, and that between them and the teeth far back there are none at all.

64

"Well, once," said Two-comes-over-the-hill, after the children nodded their heads, "both jaws of the Deer-person were filled with teeth like those he has to-day. Only the ones that are missing were many times larger and much sharper. They grew where he has no teeth to-day.

"When People possess better weapons than their neighbors they are apt to be wicked. They seek quarrels with those who are not so able to defend themselves. Fine weapons often make People bad. They made the Deer bad, as you shall see.

"One day Skinkoots was sleeping in a thicket of small firs. He had been hunting all the night before, and, of course, he had to sleep some time, so when the Sun came into the forest he made his bed and slept.

"The Blue Jay saw him and tried to wake him up, but he could not. The Pine-squirrel scolded him, but Skinkoots did not hear a word she said. Finally the Magpie-person spied him lying there

65

in the fir thicket and flew down to see if he had any meat she could steal. The Magpie-person did not make any noise. Oh, no, she thinks too much of Skinkoots to do that, for when he kills meat he is a careless Person, and will go away from it; then Magpie has a feast. Now she tip-toed around him, cocking her pretty head on one side, then on the other side, but without disturbing him. Oh, no. 'He is a good Person,' she whispered, 'I will fly away and let him sleep.'

"But Skinkoots is not always a good Person. Sometimes he kills for fat alone, and then when he has eaten the fat he will leave his kill and kill again for more fat. This is wicked, killing for fat alone.

"Bad as the Mountain-lion is, he will not do this. He kills for meat, and never leaves it until he has eaten all. He sleeps near his kill, and before he sleeps, often covers it with leaves and sticks. When nothing is left but the bones, he will sometimes even cover these before he goes away. He is a careful Person, while, in this, Skinkoots is careless.

"To-day Skinkoots slept until the Sun was in the middle of the sky. Everybody was stirring except him and *Co*-pee, the Owl-person, and the Winds. Many saw Skinkoots, but nobody disturbed him until the Deer-person came along.

"'Oh, ho! There he is!' he said to himself. 'I have been looking for him all day!' Up went his white tail, and the hair on his neck bristled till it looked like the Porcupine-person. He bounded high in the air, once, twice, three times, his mouth wide open to kill Skinkoots with his teeth and sharp hoofs.

"Thud! Thud! Thud! The Deer-person's feet struck the ground. Oh, ho! The noise wakened Skinkoots. He saw what was going on. Oh, ho! He sprang straight at the Deer-person and caught him in the mouth. His teeth were not so sharp, but they were stronger, and he twisted hard! Oh, ho! Out came all the

Deer-person's teeth except those in front and the few that are behind.

"Oh, ho! All the Deer's teeth between those in front and those far back were twisted out by Skinkoots, who held on tight.

"The Deer dragged him, and struck at him, and bawled, but Skinkoots would not let go.

"'Promise to be afraid,' he said. 'Promise to be afraid, and I will let you go.'

"'Ouch!' He was hurting the Deer-person. 'Ba, baaa!' he cried. 'I will be afraid. Let go! Let go!'

"At last Skinkoots *did* let go, and the Deer-person ran away to hide. He kept his promise. He *was* afraid. He has been afraid ever since that day, and he always will be afraid.

"You may know that what I have told you is true, for even to this day the mark of Skinkoots's teeth is on every Deer that lives. It is the black mark that encircles the under-jaw near its point. It is there to remind the Deer of his promise to be afraid. You may see this mark if you will look.

"Ho!"

"Now I must tell you that the Deer-person was so much afraid of Skinkoots that he grew poorer and poorer. He hid by day and he hid by night until he was so poor the Winds were sorry for him.

"'Go out and eat,' the South Wind told him.
"'Go out and eat. I will watch while you fill up. If any Person is looking for you when I am blowing I will tell you. Keep your head toward me and I will not lie.'

"Then the West Wind promised the same, and the East Wind promised the same, and the North Wind promised the same.

"Oh, ho! Now the Deer-person had helpers that never lied to him. He trusted them then and he does to this day. No matter what others may tell him, he believes the Winds first. If every Person on this World told the Deer *one* thing, and the Winds told him *another* thing, he would believe the thing the Winds told him.

"Now it was Skinkoots's turn to be hungry. He could not find the Deer-person. He hunted the hills, and the bottoms, and the thickets, but always the Winds told the Deer-person that Skinkoots was coming, so that he could run away. Oh, ho! Skinkoots was hungry now. He learned that the Winds were helping the Deer-person. Oh, ho! This made him angry! He pointed his arrow at the Winds and sang his war-song.

"Oh, ho! Just then he saw something sitting on a rock.

"'That is a funny-looking Person,' he said. 'I will go and see what is going on.'

"He trotted along till he came to the Person sitting on the rock. The Person wore a queer war-bonnet, and sat with his hands over his eyes. The bonnet was white and smelled so good that Skinkoots took a bite of it. Oh, ho! It was *fat*. The bonnet was made of *fat*.

"'This is good!' said Skinkoots. 'I will take another bite, I guess.' And he did!

"'Hey, you!' growled the Person, sitting up. 'What are you doing? You have torn my war-bonnet!'

"The Person was *Old*-man. Oh, ho! He had changed himself into the Winds and sat there on that rock with his hands over his eyes.

"'What is the matter? Why do you sit here this way?' asked Skinkoots, looking at the queer war-bonnet again.

"'Oh, my eyes are gone!' said *Old*-man. 'I cannot see where I am going. That is all.'

"'Well! That is *bad*,' said Skinkoots. 'But things are pretty bad with me, too. The Winds are helping the Deer-person, and I cannot get near him. I am hungry all the time now.'

"*Old*-man kept his hands over his eyes, and rocked himself. His eyes hurt him.

"Skinkoots was sorry. He liked *Old*-man, and he wanted to help him. 'I know what to do,' he said, slipping away to a huckleberry-bush, where he picked two berries and came back.

"'Take your hands away from your eyes,' he said. 'I guess I can fix you.'

"*Old*-man lifted his hands and Skinkoots stuck the two huckleberries in his head. 'There! Can you see now?' he asked.

"'Yes,' said *Old*-man, looking around. 'I can see now, and I will pay you for this. I will help you!

"'I know the Winds are helping the Deer-persons. I know all about it. Here! Take this Medicine-arrow and go away. You can kill the Deer-persons with this arrow. But you must ˉnever kill more than *two*. If you do, something will happen to you.'

"Skinkoots took the Medicine-arrow and went hunting. He was lucky. He grew fat. Then he forgot what *Old*-man had told him and killed more than two. Oh, ho! Then he lost his Medicine-arrow. But that is another story.

"Ho!"

VIII

COYOTE'S ADVENTURES

A LONG time ago there was an Old Woman-person, and she had two children that lived with her. The Old Woman-person had a hard time to make her living. Often the children cried for meat when she had no meat to give them.

One day when they were crying the Old Woman-person said: "Listen! Kingfisher is your uncle. He makes his living easily. You had better leave me and go to his lodge to live."

This was good talk. But another Person heard it. Oh, ho! Skinkoots was sitting outside the lodge door and heard what the Old Woman-person said.

"I might as well do that myself," he thought. "The Kingfisher-person is a *cousin* of mine, and

73

he ought to be glad to see me. I had better start and beat those children there."

He *did* start — and he *did* beat the children there. Kingfisher was glad to see him, of course, but he told Skinkoots that just then he had no Fishes to feed him.

"You wait here, Cousin," he said, "while I go fishing. I will be back soon." Then he put on his big war-bonnet that kills the Fish, and went away.

Skinkoots slept, for he was tired. When he wakened there was Kingfisher with a lot of Fishes.

"May I eat as many as I need? May I eat them *all?*" asked Skinkoots, looking at Kingfisher's big war-bonnet that was hanging up to dry.

"Of course," said Kingfisher. "I can get plenty more with my big war-bonnet."

Skinkoots ate every Fish, but he could not keep his eyes away from Kingfisher's war-bonnet. The weather was cold and the frost had made the feathers on the big war-bonnet look like spears — and they were spears, of course. But Skinkoots did not know this.

"Well, I am full now," said Skinkoots, licking his chops. "I could not hold another Fish; and, besides, they are all gone."

"Say," he asked, as though he had just thought of it, "why do you not visit us — my Woman and me? We are your relations."

"Well, I might," said the Kingfisher-person, "if there is a river where you live."

"River!" laughed Skinkoots. "We live beside the biggest river in this world. Come with me. And bring your war-bonnet, Cousin. There are big Fishes in that river that runs past our lodge."

Kingfisher-person took down his war-bonnet and followed Skinkoots to his lodge.

"Oh, now what shall we do?" said Skinkoots's Woman when they had seated themselves by the fire. "There is no meat to feed our Cousin."

"I will fix it," said Skinkoots. "Say, Cousin,

let me take your war-bonnet, and I will show you some *big* Fishes when I come back here."

Kingfisher said "All right," and Skinkoots took it and went out. He had watched King-fisher fishing. He had seen him dive from the limb of a tree and with his big war-bonnet catch Fishes in the rivers. But he did not know how to wear the bonnet. Oh, ho! He put it on wrong side up. He put the big war-bonnet on his head with the *spears down!*

Then he went to the big river and climbed into a tree that leaned over the water. In no time at all he saw a big Fish! Swow! Skinkoots dove! Oh, ho!

He was dead! Skinkoots was dead! The spears on the Kingfisher-person's big war-bonnet had stuck into his head. He was dead. Oh, ho!

Kingfisher and Skinkoots's Woman, who was a Dog-person, waited and waited. When her Man did not come, the Woman went out to hunt for him. She found him dead on a cake of ice, floating along.

The Woman cried, and Kingfisher came to her. "This is funny," he said, taking back his big war-bonnet. "Does he do this thing often?"

"No. This is the first time," she answered. "I suppose he saw you do this thing, and of course he had to try it. He always tries everything. I will take him to our lodge and warm him by our fire. Then he will be all right again," said the Woman.

Kingfisher put on his big war-bonnet and went fishing while the Woman carried Skinkoots to the lodge and brought him back to life.

"I am hungry," said Skinkoots when he opened his eyes to see what was going on.

Just then Kingfisher came in with his Fishes, and they had a big feast. After they had eaten, Skinkoots's Woman went to sleep, and the Kingfisher-person went to sleep. When they snored Skinkoots went out and began travelling to see what was going on.

At last he came to a Person's lodge. He heard talking inside and sat down by the door to listen.

An Old Woman was saying to her children: "If you were smart you would go and live with your uncle, the Moose-person. He makes his living easily. He always has food."

"Oh, ho!" thought Skinkoots. "I might as well do that myself. I know the Moose-person, and he ought to be glad to see me. Here I go, before those children start."

"How, Moose-person!" he said, going right into the Moose's lodge.

"How! How!" said the Moose-person. "I am sorry, but I have nothing for you to eat in here. Wait by my fire and talk to my Woman while I send our children out to get two roots."

The children brought two roots, and the Moose-person threw them into the lodge-fire.

In no time at all they were marrow-bones roasted fine.

"Eat," said the Moose-person.

And Skinkoots ate every scrap, and began to look around for more.

The Moose-person noticed this and said to his

78

wife: "Come here, Woman. We need meat for our visitor. Come over here!"

She came to her Man, and he reached out with his knife and cut off a piece of her nose. It is that way to this day, and now you know why.

The Moose-woman cried a little, and her Man put ashes on her nose. They stuck there — and that is why the nose of the Moose looks as it does to-day.

"Here, you Skinkoots, eat this meat," said the Moose-person, handing him the piece of his Woman's nose, after he had cooked it a little.

"Now, I am full," laughed Skinkoots, licking his chops. "Why do you not visit us, my Woman and me?"

"Well, I might, I suppose," said the Moose-person.

"I could not eat any more now, and, besides, there is no more to eat," said Skinkoots. "Let us start. My Woman will be glad to see you, Moose-person."

When Skinkoots and the Moose-person got to

the lodge͙ Skinkoots's Woman said: "Oh, what shall we do? There is no meat to feed our visitor."

"I will fix it," said Skinkoots. "Stay here, Moose-person, while I send our children for two roots."

When the children brought the roots, Skinkoots tossed them into the fire. But they just burned up. They were wood, and burned to ashes!

"Come here, Woman," said Skinkoots. "We need meat to feed our visitor. Come over here."

She came to her Man, and he reached out with his knife and cut off a piece of her nose. That is why the Dog's nose is shorter than the Coyote's to this day.

"Ki — aah — ah," she cried. Then Skinkoots threw ashes on his Woman's bloody nose. But she kept on crying "Ki — aah — ah" till the Moose-person asked:

"Does he do this often?"

"No. This is the first time he has tried this thing. But I suppose he saw you do it, and he had to try it. He always tries everything."

The Moose-person was sorry for her. He went out and got two roots himself. He cooked them in the fire, and they turned to marrow-bones. When they had eaten them, the Moose-person cut off a piece of his own nose, and put ashes on the cut place.

"See?" he asked. "Now my nose will look like my Woman's nose. Ours will be cut-off noses from now on. They will be *different* noses." Then he went away from there.

When he was gone Skinkoots went to sleep. He was full, and he slept late. Before he opened his eyes he heard his Woman say to his children: "Why do you not go to your uncle, the Mountain-lion-person? He is never hungry. He kills Deer easily."

"Oh, ho!" thought Skinkoots, pretending to be still asleep. "That is good talk. I will do that myself before my children do it. The

Mountain-lion-person is a kind of relation of mine, and he ought to be glad to see me."

The Mountain-lion-person had a Woman and a Boy and a Girl who lived with him. His lodge was in the cedar country and it was always dark in there. He had dried meat, and he had fresh meat, and he had some meat that was neither dry nor fresh. He had meat hanging all around his lodge, for he does not waste it. Besides, he is a Hating-person, and never gives any person anything. That is the kind of a Man *he* is.

Skinkoots found the lodge of the Mountain-lion-person. He could smell it far off. When he got there he sat down and said: "Yip, Yip, Yahhh!" four times. But nobody answered nor looked out of the lodge.

"Yip, Yip, Yahhh!" he said again, and then the Mountain-lion-person put out his fire. He did not wish for visitors. That is the kind of Man *he* is.

Skinkoots crept up to the lodge and peeked inside. "My!" he said to himself, "there is a lot of meat in this Person's lodge. I guess I will go and get my things and move here."

When he got back to his lodge he said to his Woman: "We are going to move to the cedar country. That Mountain-lion-person has more meat than he needs. He gave me lots of it, more than we can eat. Hurry, and get your things."

He took all his things, and his Woman and children followed him to the cedar country, and it was dark in there.

"See that lodge?" he said, putting down his things.

"Yes," said his Woman, afraid of the smell of the Mountain-lion-person.

"Well, that is the place. Go in there and get what that Person gave me! You tell him I sent you for it!"

The Woman did not want to go, but he made her do it. So she went inside, and, being afraid to speak, she reached for some meat that hung on the lodge-poles.

"Here, you," growled the Mountain-lion-person. "What are you doing in my lodge?"

"Is this what you gave my Man yesterday?" she asked, her voice shaking like the leaves when the Winds blow.

"No! Get out!" snarled the Lion-person. And he struck her — struck his own cousin. That is the kind of Man *he* is.

She ran out of the lodge screaming: "He struck me! He struck me!" And then she fell down.

Oh, ho! Now Skinkoots was angry. He went to his things and got out his bow and Medicine-arrow — the one *Old*-man gave him that day when he was the Winds and sat on that rock.

"I will fix that Person," he told his Woman. Then he ran to the lodge door and shot all the Lion-persons dead!

"Come here!" he called to his Woman, when the Mountain-lion-person had died. "Come here, and help me drag these dead Persons out of here."

The Woman helped him, of course, and then

"Here, you," growled the Mountain-lion-person. "What are you doing in my lodge?"

Skinkoots said: "This is a good lodge. We will live here. Bring in our children."

That night his Woman said: "Raise the door and call the Deer-persons. The Lion-person always did this. They will believe that yours is the Lion-person's voice, and will come. But when you call, you must kill the *first* one that comes and the *last* one that comes. Do not kill any Deer that come between the *first* and the *last;* remember this."

Skinkoots did as his Woman told him. He raised the lodge door and called the Deer. When they came he killed only the first one and the last one. By doing things this way he always had enough, just enough! But one night he thought: "Oh, I will kill a few more this time. There are too many, anyway."

So when he called and the Deer came crowding around, he shot and shot and shot till all his arrows were gone.

"There!" he said. "Now I shall have all the fat I want to eat, I guess."

But in the morning there were only two dead Deer lying on the ground outside.

"This is funny," said Skinkoots. "I shot many Deer last night. I wonder what is going on here."

That night when he went to bed he heard somebody crying. He sat up and listened. Now *two* were crying in the cedar country, and it was dark in there.

"Woman!" he called. "Listen! What is that crying out there?"

His Woman sat up. Oh, ho! Now *many* Persons were crying in the cedar country, and it was darker than ever in there.

"The Deer are crying," said his Woman. "They are many. You have wounded them with your arrows, and I am afraid."

Now Skinkoots heard footsteps in the cedar country. The Deer-chief was coming to see why the Mountain-lion-person had shot so many of his People. Skinkoots heard him walk close to the lodge, heard him whistle when he saw the dead Lion-person lying on the ground, and then he heard the Deer-chief run away.

"Now you have done it," said Skinkoots's Woman, tying down the lodge door. "The Deer-persons know that the Mountain-lion never kills more than he needs. They will come now and we shall die. Now you have done it!"

"What is that?" she asked, as a great rock struck a cedar-tree near the lodge. Oh, ho! The Deer-persons had climbed a mountain and were rolling big rocks down on the lodge.

Oh, ho! A big rock struck it — Swow! and crushed Skinkoots's Woman and the children. They were dead!

Before Skinkoots could grab his things another rock knocked the lodge into pieces. Oh, ho!

And now Skinkoots was running away for his life. He ran and ran until he came to a great river. Then he changed himself into a Flat Log and rolled in. The river carried him along till he saw three Old Women on the bank. They had a Salmon-fish, which they had caught in the water.

Then Skinkoots looked about him and saw a Fish-trap that covered the whole bottom of the great river. The trap was full of Salmon. All the Salmon-fish in the world were in the Fish-trap which the three Old Women had built.

"What is going on here? These Old Women-persons will starve everybody," said Skinkoots, going a little nearer the shore.

Just then one of the Old Women waded out and took hold of the Flat Log. "I want this to cut up my Fish on," she said, and carried the Flat Log to their lodge.

She laid her Salmon-fish upon the Flat Log and went back to the river for water.

As soon as she went out Skinkoots changed himself into a Baby and was crawling about the lodge when the three Old Women came in.

"Oh, look!" cried one of the Old Women. "There is a Baby here! Some Person's Baby is in our lodge!" And she began to dance.

They were glad. "Let us go and pick some berries for this Baby," they said.

When they were gone to pick the berries, Skinkoots said: "There is something going on here. These Old Women are holding all the Salmon-fish in their trap. People will starve. I must go and break their Fish-trap."

He sang his war-song. Oh, ho! There was no Baby in the lodge now! The Person was Skinkoots, himself. "Here I go to break that trap, so People will not starve," he said.

He ran down to the great river and broke the trap of the Old Women. He let nearly all the Salmon-fish out. He left a few in the trap for the Old Women, and started driving the rest down the river ahead of him! Whenever he passed a village and saw a Fish-trap he told some of the Salmon to go into it. And they did that.

The rest he drove on down the river, so there would always be Salmon-fish for People to eat.

Ho!

IX

OLD–MAN AND THE THUNDER–BIRDS

WALKS–IN–THE–WATER put wood on the fire. Then he filled and lighted a black-stone pipe with a burning twig. Drawing four deep drafts of the fragrant smoke of the kinnikinic through the long stem, he passed the pipe to Two-comes-over-the-hill, who smoked with his eyes on the crackling fire.

The children waited, speaking to each other in low voices till their grandfather returned the black-stone pipe to Walks-in-the-water. Then they were still again.

"The white frost has come," said Two-comes-over-the-hill, drawing his robe about his aged shoulders. "*Old*-man has painted the leaves, and they will soon dance with the North Wind. The season when the Thunder-birds visit us has gone. They will come no more until the leaves are green again. They were wicked Persons when this world was young. But now they do not make war unless they know that People have spoken against them. It is bad to speak ill of the Thunders. Yes, or even to think bad thoughts of them, for thinking bad thoughts is the same as speaking them aloud. And the Thunders hear our thoughts. Remember this.

"Listen! One fine morning in the Summertime, when only *Old*-man and the Persons lived on this world, Skinkoots was looking for a Rabbit-person to eat. His eyes are sharp, but the Rabbit-persons that live in this country change their robes with the seasons. In the winter-time they are white to be like the snow, and only their eyes are black. When the snow has gone away these Rabbit-persons wear brown to be like the country they live in, and then their tails are black. They are not like their cousins that live on the plains without changing their tails, even if they do change their robes. So our Rabbit-persons are always hard to see in any season. Their tails never give them away.

"Of course Skinkoots has a fine nose to help his eyes, and very soon he got his breakfast. Just as he had finished and was washing his face with his tongue, he heard something coming.

"'Oh, ho!' he said; 'what is *going on here?* I guess I will get the wind of what is coming. Then I will know quick enough. My nose will tell me the truth.'

"He soon reached a spot where the Wind — there was only a little — told him what he wanted to know. And then he began to laugh and dance.

"'Oh, ho!' he said, standing on his hind legs, 'Oh, ho! It is *Nu-la-kin-nah* that is coming. Oh, ho!'

"He had learned 'Oh, ho' from *Old*-man, and he liked to say it. He thought it sounded fine, so he said it often.

"'Now I am glad!' he laughed, trotting to meet his friend. 'I thought it might be the Mountain-lion-person that was coming, and I don't like that Person. He is a stingy Person.

When he has killed meat, he will not let me have even a bite. Well, I am glad that it is not the Lion-person that is coming.'

"Finally Skinkoots stopped and began to laugh. 'What a foolish Person I am to be travelling to meet a Person who is coming toward me. I will wait here. Why did n't I think of this before? My legs will last longer.'

"He sat down and waited till *Old*-man came along, his keen nose telling him what other Persons were doing where the Wind came from.

"'How, *Nu-la-kin-nah!*' he said, when *Old*-man was about to pass without seeing him.

"'Hey, you Skinkoots, I have been looking for you!' laughed *Old*-man, leaning on his staff.

"'Well, now you have found me. What is going on where you have been?'

"'I have not *been* any place. I am just *going* there.'

"'Where?' asked Skinkoots, sniffing the Wind.

"'*Everywhere*, of course, and I want you to come along.'

"'Well, all right. I have not anything to do. I will go!' said Skinkoots. And so they began travelling together — *Old*-man ahead and Skinkoots behind.

"Of course *Old*-man talked a good deal without saying much that was worth while, and maybe this is the reason that Skinkoots did not remember what came to his ears. When a Person talks all the time, one grows tired of waiting for smart words among so many that are foolish. It is like waiting for birch-leaves in a cottonwood grove when the Fall Winds are blowing.

"But *Old*-man thought Skinkoots was listening when he said: 'Say, you Skinkoots, we shall soon come to a dead Pine-tree. It stands alone on a high hill and there is a bad cliff beneath it. The Pine-tree's top is broken off, and its trunk has no limbs. This Tree is very tall, and on its broken-off top there is a nest — a very large nest built of heavy sticks as big as my arms. When we come close to this Tree we shall hear queer noises, but you must not listen to these noises. When you hear them you must not look up to learn who is making the noises. Keep your eyes straight ahead of you and pass on as though you heard nothing at all.'

"*Old*-man's words were plain enough. Any Person could understand them if he were listening. But Skinkoots had closed his ears. Besides, he stopped to eat a Mouse-person and got a little behind *Old*-Man.

"The Sun was right over the Broken-off-pine-tree when they came to it and sure enough Skinkoots heard queer noises. They came from the nest in the Broken-off-pine.

"'Kin-nak-nak-kin! Kin-nak-nak-kin-ahhh-ooo-eee-ah!'

"'What is going on up there, I wonder?' said Skinkoots, stopping to look up.

"The Sun was in his eyes and he had to shade them with his hand. Then he looked up again, and saw the big nest on the Broken-off-pine. But he did not know what Persons lived there.

Oh, no, he did not even guess, or he would not have looked at all.

"'Kin-nak-nak-kin! Kin-nak-nak-kin-ahhh-ooo-eee-ah!' Two great black Bird-persons were sitting on the nest making these queer noises. But Skinkoots did not know what Persons they were. He did not even guess that they were children of the Thunder-birds that sat on the big nest.

"'Kin-nak-nak-kin! Kin-nak-nak-kin-ahhh-ooo-eee-ah!'

"'I like that,' said Skinkoots, listening. 'I think I can do it myself! Oh, ho! I know I can do it!' Then he made the queer noise himself. Once, twice, three times he made it — and Swow! He found himself in the big nest with the young Thunder-birds. And so did *Old*-man, who had nothing at all to do with making that noise.

"'Now see what you have done, Skinkoots!' cried *Old*-man, hanging onto the nest with both hands, for up there the Wind was blowing and the Broken-off-tree rocked frightfully.

"'Now see what you have done! We cannot climb down because we cannot get to the tree trunk from this nest. Those Thunder-birds will be coming along to look after their children. They will kill us. Didn't I tell you —' began *Old*-man.

"'Yes, *Nu-la-kin-nah;* yes, you told me, I guess. But I did not hear you,' whined Skinkoots, hanging on for dear life. 'Next time I will listen, *Nu-la-kin-nah* — next time I will listen.'

"'Oh, you will, will you? Well, then, listen now, Skinkoots, while I talk to these young Thunders.

"'Say, you Black-persons, when does your mother come home?' he asked.

"'When it rains,' said both Black-persons together.

"'And when does your father come?'

"'When it hails,' said both Black-persons together.

"'Oh, I see,' said *Old*-man.

"'Yes, and when our father and mother are home we are all here.'

97

"'Oh, I see,' said *Old*-man.

"'Listen, Skinkoots, you Foolish-person. When their mother comes she will ask us: "Which of you two gets tired first?" Remember this, for you must answer her and say: "My friend gets tired first. I never, never get tired myself." Then you must get up and dance to prove it.'

"'Dance!' whined Skinkoots. 'It is all I can do to stay in this nest, big as it is. How can I dance when I have to hang on?'

"'Well, you *must* dance. That is all. And I will tell you another thing, Skinkoots; if you live through the first dance, you will have to dance again when the father comes home. So get ready!'

"'Oh, dear! Look!' whispered Skinkoots, pointing toward the West.

"'Oh, ho!' said *Old*-man. 'Oh, ho! She comes, I guess — the mother of these two Black-persons. Get ready to dance, Skinkoots!'

"Skinkoots looked wildly about. His ears

were flat down on his head, but there was no place to hide. 'Oh, dear!' he whimpered miserably.

"Then he looked toward the West again. Oh, ho! The little black spot he had seen there was growing! Oh, ho!

"Now the Winds came to shake the Broken-off-tree until it cracked. Oh, ho! The sky grew black over their heads, and the Thunders rolled, and the lightning flashed, and there were smells of things burning, when suddenly the great nest tilted frightfully. She was there beside them — the Mother Thunder-bird. Oh, ho! She was there in the nest.

"'What is this? Meat to eat! Good!' she said. 'I will fix it for you, children.'

"'Now, tell me, which of you gets tired first?' she asked, turning her awful eyes upon *Old*-man and Skinkoots.

"Just then the Wind whistled loud, and *Old*-man nudged Skinkoots. 'Get up — get up and tell her!' he whispered. 'Tell her I am the one;

and then dance to prove it. Quick, Skin-koots!'

"Skinkoots sprang to his feet and began to dance. 'I never get tired — my friend is always that way,' he said, hopping all around the nest.

"'Well, that is enough dancing. Sit down,' said the Mother Thunder-bird. And Skinkoots was glad of the chance, of course.

"'So you are the one that gets tired first,' said the great Black Bird, looking at *Old*-man, who was sitting with his back against the side of the nest.

"'He says so,' grunted *Old*-man, as though Skinkoots might have lied.

'Well, I believe it, anyway. Stretch out your legs. I always begin on the legs when I eat Persons.'

"Skinkoots's eyes were popping from his head when *Old*-man calmly stretched out his legs as the Mother Thunder-bird had told him.

"But just when the wicked Black Bird had

opened her mouth to take hold of his feet *Old*-man stabbed her with his knife, and she died!

"'Now, Skinkoots, quick! Help me roll her over the side of this nest before her Man comes home. He will be harder to fool than she was, but he will ask the same question, and you must do just as you did before. Ho! Ho! Ho!' Over the side of the big nest went the Mother Thunder-bird, and they heard her body strike the ground. It was as though a pine-tree had fallen from a mountain-top.

"'Oh! Look, *Nu-la-kin-nah!*' cried Skinkoots. 'He is coming already. Oh, dear. What shall I do?'

"'Do? I have told you what to do; and see that you do it. Sit down now and rest.'

"A great black cloud that had red on its edges was coming fast. There was deep Thunder and the Winds nearly tipped over the Broken-off-tree. Lightning ripped a tall pine to splinters, and both *Old*-man and Skinkoots were hanging on for their lives when it began to hail. Oh, ho!

The hailstones were like the eggs of the Goose-person! The air grew cold as Winter, and the hailstones were up to *Old*-man's shoulders as he sat in the nest. Oh, ho!

"Then suddenly, as though somebody had kindled a fire in a dark lodge, the sun came out of the clouds — and there, beside them in the nest, was the Father Thunder-bird!

"His head was red, and his angry eyes were green as the grass in summer.

"'What is this? Meat to eat? Good! I will fix it for you, children,' he said.

"'Now tell me which of you gets tired first,' he asked, turning his greedy eyes on *Old*-man and then on little Skinkoots.

"This time Skinkoots did not wait. '*He* does,' he said, dancing around on the hailstones in the nest. '*He* does. *I* never get tired, myself.'

"'Well, that is enough dancing. Sit down!' said the Father Thunder-bird. And Skinkoots was glad of the chance, of course.

"'So you are the one that gets tired first, hey?' said the wicked Black Bird to *Old*-man, who was sitting among hailstones that were nearly up to his shoulders.

"'Well, stretch out your legs. I always begin on the legs when I eat Persons.'

"*Old*-man stretched out his legs quick enough; but just when the Father Thunder-bird stooped to take *Old*-man's feet in his mouth he stabbed him, and he died.

"'Say — that was easy,' laughed *Old*-man, rising. 'Here, Skinkoots, help me roll him out of this nest. I know what I shall do next. Hurry!'

"They tugged and they pulled and they lifted until over went the great Black Bird to the hail-covered ground. It was as though two great pine-trees had fallen from a mountain-top when he struck the earth — Swow! Even the hill trembled.

"And now the Thunder-birds' children began to cry. It was not like the crying of other Persons. It was like the screaming of a hundred women who are frightened.

"'Stop it!' cried *Old*-man. 'Stop it at once, or I will kill you as I did your parents.

"'Listen to me!' he said when the children were still. 'You young ones must take us down to the ground on your backs. Get up here!'

"The two young Thunder-birds got up, and *Old*-man climbed on one, while Skinkoots got on the other.

"'All ready now,' said *Old*-man, grabbing a handful of neck-feathers. 'You two birds be careful what you do, or you will be sorry.'

"Oh, ho! Away they went, but *up, up, up,* almost to the sky. Then suddenly both the Birds turned downward, and *Old*-man felt safer when he saw the trees beneath him. *Down, down, down* came the black Thunder-birds until *Old*-man could count the hailstones. *Down, down,* until he was almost to the ground.

"And then, just as he stepped off the Bird's

back, Skinkoots said: 'Kin-nak-nak-kin — Kin-nak-nak-kin-ahhh-ooo-eee-ah!'

"Oh, ho! Up went the Thunder-bird again, with Skinkoots on his back. *Up, up, up* into the clouds. *Old*-man held onto *his* Bird, so he could not fly. They tumbled and rolled and mussed up the hailstones, but *Old*-man held on tight until the Bird gave up — and said so.

"'Good!' said *Old*-man, out of breath from everything. 'Good! Now you make that queer noise, yourself! Make it good and loud, too. I want your brother up there to hear it, and bring Skinkoots back here. *Make* it, I tell you!'

"'Kin-nak-nak-kin — Kin-nak-nak-kin-ahhh-ooo-eee-ah!' shrieked the Thunder-bird, now badly frightened.

"'Good!' said *Old*-man. 'Now make it again — and make it louder this time.'

"Oh, ho! the voice of the Thunder-bird made *Old*-man's head dizzy, but he hung on till the other Thunder-bird came sailing down to the ground with Skinkoots safe on his back.

"'Now, you listen, Skinkoots,' said *Old*-man, when Skinkoots stepped upon the ground. 'You hold that Bird-person tight. Do not let him get away until I kill him. I have already killed mine. Now I will kill yours. Hold him, Skinkoots!'

"'Well, hurry!' gasped Skinkoots. 'He is hard to hold, I can tell you. Oh! ouch! Hurry, *Nu-la-kin-nah!*'

"*Old*-man ran to the floundering Skinkoots, and stabbed the Thunder-bird with his knife. Once, twice, three times he stabbed the black Thunder-bird that Skinkoots held; and when *Old*-man's knife struck the third time something happened.

"Oh, ho! The eyes of the Thunder-bird burst! 'Pop!' they went, and out of the eyeholes flew *two* Birds that were no bigger than crows.

"'Hey, you Bird-persons, listen!' said *Old*-man.

"The Birds listened, of course, and *Old*-man

said: 'From this day onward you two shall be Thunder-birds. But you must not kill People who do not speak bad words against you. Now go on about your business and do not visit this world in Winter-time.'

"They have remembered what *Old*-man told them. This is why the Thunder-birds do no great harm to-day. Besides, they do not come here in winter.

"Ho!"

X

WAR WITH UP–THERE–PERSONS

A YOUNG Woman lived alone in a lodge, because she was a widow. Her husband, the Muskrat, had died.

One day the Woman's dead husband's younger brother came to the young Woman's lodge and asked her to marry him.

But she would not, and this younger Muskrat killed her because she would not marry him. He shot her with a *different* arrow, and went away from the lodge.

A Person found the dead young Woman and called: "This Woman is dead. She has been killed with a *different* arrow."

All the other Persons came to look. "Ahh!" they said; "she is dead. Whose arrow is this? It is a *different* arrow!"

Nobody knew.

"Get the Frog," said Skinkoots. "She has

been all over this world. She will know whose arrow killed this young Woman. Go get her."

A Person went for the Frog and she came to the lodge and looked.

"Whose arrow is that, Frog-woman?" asked Skinkoots.

"I do not know," answered the Frog-woman, taking the arrow in her hands. "I do not know."

But she *did* know. She knew the arrow belonged to her grandson, but she would not tell on him. She only said, "I do not know," and went away with the arrow.

"There must be a Country in the Sky," said the Wolverene. "Persons must live there. They have shot this young Woman. It was one of *their* arrows that killed her. Let us go to war with those Up-there-persons."

"How shall we get there?" somebody asked him. And then there was much talking.

"I know," said a Person who could shoot far. "Watch me!"

He bent his bow and let his arrow fly upward. Everybody heard its point strike something out of sight in the clouds. Oh, ho! His arrow struck something up there, and while the rest murmured, the Person shot *another* arrow, and it *struck* and *stuck* in the notch of the *first*. He shot all his arrows and each stuck in the other's notch until when his last arrow was gone the other Persons could see it sticking through the clouds.

Then they all began to shoot arrows; many, many arrows, and each one stuck in the notch of the one before it, until the string of arrows reached *nearly* to the ground.

"Keep on — keep on!" called Skinkoots. But all the arrows were used; all had been shot away. Oh, ho!

"Now what shall we do?" asked Skinkoots. "We could go up there on that arrow-trail if it reached the ground."

"I will take care of that," said the Raven-person. "I will take care of that." And he stuck his beak under the last arrow that nearly touched the ground!

Oh, ho! Now the arrow-trail reached the ground. The Raven's beak was all that was needed.

"Come on! Let us start up," said Skinkoots.

"Wait for me," begged Old Man-wolverene. "I have to put away my things. I shall be back in a day or two. I thought of this thing. Wait for me."

But they grew tired of waiting, and climbed up, up, up until they were all in the clouds. Yes, they left Old Man-wolverene and went up.

Muskrat was far ahead, and when he got there he made a Lake and many lodges. His many lodges looked like a village in the clouds. At last the other Persons got there and began to make war on the lodges. They tipped over one, and a Left-handed-person walked out.

They shot him, and tipped over another lodge, and out came the Left-handed-one again. They

111

shot him, and tipped over another lodge. Out walked the Left-handed-person again.

"Hold on!" cried Skinkoots. "I guess he is always the same One. Do not shoot him any more."

Then they ran back to go down the way they came up. But the arrow trail was gone.

Oh, ho! Old Man-wolverene had come back and found that they had not waited until he put away his things. He was angry. "I will fix those Persons," he said, and he tore down the arrow trail, so that the other Persons could not reach the earth.

"Now what shall we do?" asked somebody getting frightened up there.

"I know," said Skinkoots. "Come with me."

They all went where he led them, and they found the place where the Thunder-bird drank. They waited there, and when he came for water they killed him and divided his feathers among them, as far as they would go. But there were not feathers enough to go around.

WAR WITH UP–THERE–PERSONS

Those that got them put them on and flew down to the earth again. But the Fish had none, and jumped anyhow. Some came through all right, but not the Sucker-person. He struck on his face and broke it. Even to-day you may see just what happened to the Sucker-person when he jumped down from the Sky. The fall made the Trout flat because he struck the ground with his side — except the Bull Trout, and he rolled a long way after he struck, so that he is long and rounder than he was.

Everybody jumped but the Bat-person and his cousin, the Flying Squirrel. They had been given no feathers, and everybody believed they would not make it. But they both nudged each other and laughed a little to see the Fishes jump, and when the last was gone the Bat-person said: "This will be easy, Cousin. We will use our own robes to fly with. Look!"

He hooked his fingers in his own robe and spread it out. Then he jumped, and came sailing down just when the poor Sucker-person's brother's widow was trying to mend Sucker-person's mouth, which she could not — and she did not do. It is that way to this day.

Now the Flying Squirrel was alone up there. "I guess I can manage," he said bravely.

Oh, ho! He pulled out his skin along his sides and held it that way. Then he jumped and came sailing down almost as easily as the Bat-person, his cousin.

He does this same thing to this day when he jumps. Yes, he just pulls out his own skin and sails. And now you know why.

Ho!

XI

THE RABBIT–PERSON

"THAT was a good story," said Little-crane, a boy of nine years. "We like it when you tell us of those Persons who lived so long ago. But tell me, Grandfather, was my father brave?"

"Yes, Little-crane, your father was brave. The Piegans killed him in a battle when you had seen but two snows. We fought hard, but the Piegans killed your father and Black Wolf and Eagle-man. It was a good fight, even though we lost it. Yes, your father was a brave man."

He smoked a while thoughtfully. "Of course," he said, laying aside his black stone pipe, "some Persons are brave. Others are cowards. *Old*-man made them to be that way. They cannot help it, even if they wished to.

"The Rabbit-person is a great coward, and everybody knows it now. But there was a time

115

when nobody knew that the Rabbit-person was afraid. Skinkoots and the Grizzly Bear found it out. And then these two told everybody. Now everybody knows it, and some People laugh. But it is wrong to laugh at the Rabbit-person. He cannot help being afraid. How can he, when *Old*-man made him that way?

"It was mean of Skinkoots and the Grizzly Bear-person to tell everybody that the Rabbit was a coward. It was especially mean of Skinkoots, who sometimes runs away, himself. It was not so bad on the part of the Grizzly Bear-person, of course, because he does not understand. He does not know how to be afraid. One can hardly blame him for laughing at a coward, since *he* always is brave. *Old*-man made him that way. He cannot help it if he wished to, you see. How can he?

"Listen! The day was cold, but there was no snow on the ground. The sky was spotted with little white clouds that were running races with each other, and sometimes the Winds blew.

THE RABBIT–PERSON

The Sun paid no attention to the little white clouds in the sky, and kept at his work of making the day bright. And it was on this *very* day that the Rabbit-person did the foolish thing that set everybody laughing at him. But nobody would have learned about it if Skinkoots and the Grizzly Bear-person had not told.

"Perhaps the Rabbit-person was not feeling well that morning when he hopped out of his lodge to find his breakfast. Anyhow, when he found what he wanted to eat he was among tall trees. No other Persons were near, and he began eating, a little here and a little there, till suddenly he heard a noise.

"Up he sat on his haunches. Up went his long ears. Oh, ho!

"'What was that, I wonder,' he whispered, his eyes looking frightened. 'What was that noise?' But now the noise was gone.

"'I guess it was only my heart beating,' thought the Rabbit-person, looking relieved. 'Yes, I guess that was what it was.'

"You see, the Rabbit-person was always a great coward, and he knew it. But nobody else did — not yet.

"He began eating again, a little here and a little there until — oh, ho! — he heard the noise again, and louder than before. 'Hark!' he said, and up he sat on his haunches again. Up went his long ears, and his nose was still for once in his life.

"'What was that?' he whispered, his head turning this way and that way.

"Just then the noise came again and louder than ever. It came from over his head. Oh, ho! The tree-tops were bending! The little clouds, running their races in the sky, were passing the forests, and, of course, the Winds were with them, watching the races.

"It was the Wind that bent the tree-tops. It was only the Wind that made the noise in the forest. Oh, ho! It was only the Wind that the Rabbit-person heard!

"'Look at that tree bending!' he whispered.

'Something will fall on me here! I shall be killed if I stay here!'

"Just then the little clouds that raced in the sky made shadows on the ground — shadows that raced through the forests as the clouds passed the Sun.

"That was enough! Oh, ho! That was *too much* for the Rabbit-person.

"Away he went, his black tail bobbing so fast that no Person could count its bobs; not even Skinkoots, who saw him go by with his long ears tight to his shoulders.

"'What is going on here?' said Skinkoots. 'Look at that Person go! He is a good runner; about the best there is, I guess. I wonder what is after him? I will run along behind and see. But I shall have to hurry.'

"He sprang out of the bushes, and away he went behind the Rabbit-person to find out what was chasing him. But he saw nobody — heard nothing at all, as he raced behind the frightened Rabbit-person, till the Grizzly Bear-person called: 'Hey, you Skinkoots-person, what is going on here?'

"'Something is after the Rabbit-person,' answered Skinkoots over his shoulder. 'I cannot stop to talk to you. Come on! Let us see who it is that is chasing him!'

"'Well, wait, can't you!' cried the Grizzly Bear-person, starting to run after Skinkoots.

"'No, of course I can't wait. Come on, you Big-person, if you think you are a runner!' laughed Skinkoots, now far ahead.

"But if anybody thinks the Grizzly Bear-person cannot run he is mistaken. He does not know that Person at all.

"Oh, ho! Now there were two that raced behind the Rabbit-person to see what it was that chased him.

"Oh, ho! Through the forests, over the hills, across the mountains, they raced, until at last they came to the plains. Oh, ho! They came to the plains.

"Skinkoots's tongue was hanging out of his

mouth and water dripped from it when he stopped to wait for the Grizzly Bear-person, who was far behind.

"'I have not seen a living thing!' gasped the Grizzly Bear-person, sitting down, for he was tired out. 'Not a living thing, not even the Rabbit-person himself. Have you?'

"'Not until I stopped to wait for you,' panted Skinkoots. 'Say, that Rabbit-person is fast, I tell you! I have not seen him since I started. If my nose had not helped me, we should not have got here. We should have lost him altogether.'

"'Lost him?' grunted the Grizzly Bear, lying down on the plains. 'I guess we have lost him all right. I do not see him anywhere. Say, but this is a flat country here. One can see all over *this* country. But I do not see that Rabbit-person.'

"'Well, I do,' said Skinkoots. 'That is why I stopped here to wait for you.'

"'Where is he?' asked the Grizzly Bear-person, sitting up on his haunches and looking all around.

"'Right over there.' Skinkoots pointed to a sage-bush. And there, almost dead from running, was the Rabbit-person, his sides going in and out, in and out, so fast you could not count them.

"'Say, do you think we can get near enough to talk to him?' asked the Grizzly Bear-person.

"'I guess so, if we sing a little,' said Skinkoots. And then he began to sing a song to show the Rabbit-person they were not at war with him.

"They both got pretty near, near enough to talk to the Rabbit-person; and Skinkoots asked: 'Say, you, what was after you that time?'

"The Rabbit's sides were still going in and out, in and out, so fast you could not count them. 'I do not know what Person it was,' he gasped. 'I was back there in the forests when a noise came. Then the trees bent, and *black things* that were nothing at all raced past me! I was afraid something would fall on me!'

"Oh, ho! It was only the Wind that had frightened the Rabbit-person. Nothing at all was after him!

"At first Skinkoots was angry when he heard this. 'Say, you,' he said, walking a little nearer, 'I ought to eat you for what you have done. But I won't — oh, no, I won't — ha-ha-ha!'

"'Did you hear what he said, Bear-person?' asked Skinkoots, out of breath with his laughing. 'Did you hear that?'

"'Yes, oh, yes, I heard. Ha-ha-ha!' The Grizzly Bear-person began to roll over on the plains. 'The *Wind frightened* him. Ha-ha! The *Wind*, Skinkoots! He said it was the Wind that scared him — the little coward.'

"Now both were laughing at the Rabbit-person, who saw nothing at all to laugh at. but looked foolish.

"'Say, Brother,' said Skinkoots, suddenly sitting up, 'I know what let's do, you and I. Let us go all over this world and tell everybody we see about this thing!'

"'All right,' agreed the Grizzly Bear-person, starting out. 'Let's go right now, Skinkoots!'

"And so they started, telling every Person they saw until everybody knew that the Rabbit-person was a coward. They did this thing to punish the Rabbit for making them run so far for nothing. That is why.

"Ho!"

XII

THE SKUNK–PERSON

THE Skunk-person lived with his brother, the Fisher-person. Skunk's brother was a good hunter. He killed the meat. Skunk packed it to camp and cut the wood, and packed the water, and he did most of the cooking besides. But Fisher was the better hunter, and so they got along.

They lived in the big forest where things are pretty still. One day when they were out of meat, and only bones were left, the Fisher-person went hunting Deer.

There was another lodge in that forest, and the Persons who lived there were always hungry. These Persons were an old Frog-woman and two Girls. The Girls were a Pine-squirrel and a Chipmunk. Both were smart, and both were pretty. These Girls had heard about the Fisher-person's hunting. They knew his brother the Skunk-person lived with him, and that he was always in camp doing a Woman's work. Nobody liked the Skunk-person very well. And these Girls did not. But they were hungry, and something had to be done about it. This is what they did.

They both went near the lodge where the Fisher and the Skunk lived, and hid themselves. They were afraid the Fisher-person might be out hunting; and he was, of course.

Thump! Thump! Thump! — Thump-thump-thump!

"Ssh!" said the Pine-squirrel-girl. "The Skunk-person is pounding bones." They climbed up on a tree, but they could not see.

Oh, ho! Skunk was breaking bones and eating the marrow. But the Girls could not see him. Thump! Thump! Thump! — Thump-thump-thump! Just then a piece of bone flew and struck a tree.

"Oh, ho!" said the Skunk-person, putting

down his stone-hammer. "There is something going on here. Somebody must be coming."

He is a smart man. He knew those Girls liked his brother. He knew they did not like him; so he got up and put on his brother's robe.

While he was doing this he let the pounding go on. *THUMP! THUMP! THUMP! — Thump-thump-thump!*

Oh, ho! He left the pounding going on, and went out with a kettle to get some water from the river.

His Medicine had told him those Girls were somewhere around there, and he wanted to fool them. He wanted to make them believe he was his brother.

Of course the pounding was going on, *THUMP! THUMP! THUMP! — Thump-thump-thump!* — and the Girls thought the Skunk's brother was back from hunting.

"Let us go in there," said the Chipmunk-girl. "Fisher-person is back. One has gone for water,

127

and I think it was the Fisher-person. Besides, there is pounding in there."

"No — no! That Person is not Fisher! That was Skunk who went for water. He is wearing his brother's robe. That is all!" said the Pine-squirrel-girl. "Wait!"

Skunk-person heard the Girls talking, and he was afraid his brother might come home, anyway. So he came running back with his kettle of water. He ran so fast he slopped it. The slopped water ran into the low places and stayed there. That is why there are so many little lakes in this country. The water the Skunk-person slopped that day made them. They are everywhere, and you may see them.

When Skunk got back to the lodge he had but little water left in his kettle. But he did not care about that. He took off his brother's robe and commenced pounding bones again. Then he began talking to his brother, who was not there.

Oh, ho! Now the Girls were fooled. They

went inside, because they wanted to marry the Fisher-person. He was a good hunter, and they wanted to be his Women. But, oh, ho! There was *Skunk!*

But he was polite to them, and he fed them some marrow. Then he hid them behind some robes, because he heard his brother coming. Oh, ho!

Of course Fisher-person knew the Girls were in there. He knew the Skunk had hidden them. His Medicine told him. He knew these things even when he killed a Deer away off in the forest, and had made up his mind what to do about it, too.

He had a rope. It was painted red, and he always gave it to his brother, Skunk-person, when he sent him out to bring in the meat he had killed.

Now he said: "Well, Brother, here is my rope. Go bring in my meat. It is all ready for you over by the mountains."

Oh, ho! Skunk took the red rope and went

out. But he did not know that Fisher had given him a *different* rope.

This red rope was only the intestines of the Deer that Fisher had killed. But Skunk did not know it.

When he was gone, Fisher-person called the Girls from behind the robes, and said: "When my brother uses that red rope it will break. When he fixes the rope it will break again. Besides, I will make other trouble for him out there. But we must work fast. He is a mean Person, and will kill us if he can.

"Now, listen. Skunk's Medicine is here," he said. "Dig under every one of these lodge-poles and you will find a bone. These bones are his Medicine, and we must get them. Hurry! Get every scrap of bone you find under the ends of these lodge-poles."

The Girls began to dig on one side of the lodge, and the Fisher-person on the other side.

Just then the Winds began to blow, and the Chipmunk-girl said: "How cold it is growing!"

THE SKUNK–PERSON

"Yes," said the Fisher. "I am making it storm on my brother. I am trying to freeze him out there while that rope keeps on breaking and making him trouble. But get those bones! They are his Medicine. If we get them all, he *will* freeze out there."

The Chipmunk-girl's fingers were getting cold. "I guess I have got all my bones out," she said, piling several near the fire. She knew she had left a little bone in the last hole she dug. But her fingers were cold, and she did not tell anybody about it.

Fisher-person burned the bones. "Are you sure you got them all, Girls?" he asked, stirring the fire.

"Yes," said the Pine Squirrel-girl honestly.

"Yes," said the Chipmunk-girl, and *she* was telling a lie. She spoke with a forkéd tongue, because her fingers were cold.

"Well, then, let us run away from here," said Fisher-person, and they went out into the forest and hid themselves to see what happened.

Skunk-person was having a hard time out there. He tied up the meat, put it on his back, and started. Then the red rope broke.

He mended it, and it broke again. He mended it, and it broke again. Then it began to storm and turn cold. The trees cracked, and *Co*-pee, the Owl, made talk when it was not yet dark.

"Oh, ho!" said Skunk-person. "*Something is going on here.* I shall leave this meat, I guess. *Something is going on here.*"

He left the broken red rope and the meat and ran back to the lodge.

The fire was out, and he smelled burned bones. "*Something is going on here,*" he said, and began to look for his Medicine. He began digging where the other Persons had dug. And there was nothing!

> " *The Chief is going to freeze,*
> *The Chief is going to freeze,*
> *The Chief is going to freeze,*
> *The Chief is going to freeze,*"

he sang — and just then he found the little bone which the Chipmunk-girl had left because her fingers were cold.

Oh, ho! He found the little bone and lay down on it. In no time at all he was warm! "I will fix those Persons in the morning," he said, and went to sleep on the little bone.

Out there in the forest where they were hiding, Fisher-person asked: "Girls, are you sure you got *all* those bones? My Medicine tells me that *something is going on here.*"

"Yes," said the Pine Squirrel-girl honestly.

"Oh, I left one little piece," said the Chipmunk-girl. "But it did not amount to anything. My fingers were cold."

"Ahhh! I knew that *something was going on here,*" said Fisher-person. "Now he will kill us, I suppose. If you know a place where we shall be safe, we had better start. I know my brother. He will go to war with us now."

They ran and ran through the forest. "Here is a good lodge," said the Chipmunk-girl, and she ran inside. It was a hole under a tree —a very small hole, of course.

"I cannot get in there," said Fisher-person. "Come on!"

They ran again till the Pine Squirrel-girl said, "Wait! here is a good lodge," and she ran inside. It was a hole in a tree that had fallen. It was not a very big hole, of course.

"I cannot get in there," said Fisher-person. "Come on!"

They ran and ran till Fisher-person said: "Here is a good lodge. It is mine." It was a hole in a big tree that was standing. Fisher went inside, and the Girls went in, too.

They thought they were safe now. But in the morning! Oh, ho! In the morning Skunk-person came to that tree, and he made such a smell around there that the tree fell down and killed the Fisher-person and both the Girls.

Yes, that tree fell down — and all the trees around there fell down when the Skunk-person made his smell. A great forest fell down that day when Skunk killed Fisher and those Girls.

Ho!

XIII

COYOTE AND BUFFALO BULL

NO Person travels more than Skinkoots. He is always travelling. He is always trying things.

One day he came to the skull of a Buffalo Bull. "Why do you not come alive?" he asked. But he did not stop.

He went on, and came to the skull again. "Why do you not come alive?" he asked. But he did not stop.

He went on till he came to the skull another time. "Why do you not come alive?" he said.

Then he spread his robe and lay down to sing a song.

> "*A mother and two children,*
> *A mother and two children,*
> *A mother and two children,*
> *A mother and two children,*"

he sang, till he heard a noise.

He jumped up, looked, listened.   But nothing was around there.

He lay down again.

> "*A mother and two children,*
> *A mother and two children,*
> *A mother and two children,*
> *A mother and two children,*"

he sang, till he heard the noise again.

He jumped up, looked, listened.   But nothing was around there.

He lay down once more.

> "*A mother and two children,*
> *A mother and two children,*
> *A mother and two children,*
> *A mother and two children,*"

he sang, till he heard that noise once more.

He jumped up, looked.   "Oh!" he said, "that Buffalo Bull-person has come alive!   He is after me!

"Come on!" he called.   "You cannot catch *me*.   I am *fast*.   You cannot catch *me!*"

"Come on!" he called. "You cannot catch me. I am fast. You cannot
catch me!"

He *was* fast. He ran away from the Bull. In no time at all he was far away, and he lay down on his robe to rest.

> "*A mother and two children,*
> *A mother and two children,*
> *A mother and two children,*
> *A mother and two children,*"

he was singing when the Bull got there.

Skinkoots jumped up with his robe, and ran like the Wind till he was far off. Then he lay down on his robe to rest again. He was singing that song when the Bull came along.

He thought he was farther away than he was, and this time the Bull got close to him before Skinkoots heard him coming.

He jumped up to run, but the Bull grabbed his robe. Oh, ho! Skinkoots ran away without his robe, and he was getting tired, too. But he ran far. He ran *farther* this time before he stopped to rest.

He had no robe now. "I know what I will do," he said. "I shall lie down where I cannot sleep. I will rest where I shall not be very comfortable."

Just then he came to a big Ant-hill. "This is just the place I was looking for," he said. "These Persons will not let me sleep, I guess." And he lay down there.

He was very tired, but of course he could not sleep on that Ant-hill. He just waited without singing that song. He thought the Bull would come. And he *did* come.

"Brrrrrr!" said the Bull. And Skinkoots was running like the Winds. Oh, ho! He was frightened now. That Bull was at war with him! Oh, ho!

Something had to be done about it! Skinkoots saw a tree ahead of him, and he ran inside the middle of that tree.

Swow! The Bull's head smashed the tree to pieces.

Out ran Skinkoots. He was not hurt, but he was afraid. He saw a big rock, and ran inside the middle of it.

Swow! The Bull's head broke the rock into pieces.

Out ran Skinkoots. He was not hurt, but he was growing more afraid. He saw a Lake, and ran into the middle of it.

The Bull saw him out there, and he stopped by the Lake. "Brrrrrr!" he said. "I will fix him now."

He began to drink the water. Oh, ho! The Bull drank the Lake.

Out ran Skinkoots. He was not hurt, but he was very much afraid. He saw some Service-berry bushes, and he ran inside the middle of the biggest stick among them.

Swow! Swow! Swow! The Bull's head bent the stick, but could not break it.

"Hey, you!" called Skinkoots. "You cannot break this Service-berry stick. You are acting foolish. We have had a lot of fun. I have beaten you, and you might as well say so. Besides, I am tired."

The Bull did not like that talk, and he pawed the ground and grumbled.

But Skinkoots said: "I will give you a new Medicine if you will smoke with me."

"I do not want any new Medicine. My Medicine is good," said the Bull.

"Well, smoke some Willow-bark with me, anyway. It will not hurt you," offered Skinkoots.

"All right," said the Bull. "I will do that." And he sat down.

Skinkoots came out of the middle of the Service-berry stick, looked for fire, but there was none around there. He offered the pipe to the Sun, and the Sun gave him fire for the Willow-bark.

"This smoke is sweet," said the Bull, when Skinkoots passed him the lighted pipe. "I like this smoke, and I want to tell you something. I am not the same Bull that owned that skull you saw over there, but I have been killed every time I passed that place — every time something happens to me right there.

"Now, you listen. I have two Women. I

want to go to them. But every time I start I get killed right there where that skull was."

"Well, that is funny," said Skinkoots. "I will tell you what I will do. I will go there with you. Where are these Women?"

"Oh, over that way," said the Bull. So they started.

At last they came to where Persons were tanning hides. A big village was there, and many warriors were near the lodges. "That is where my Women are," said the Bull. "I guess it is a pretty Bad Place, too."

"Well, you go and get those Women of yours. I will wait for you," said Skinkoots, sitting down.

The Bull went into the village and got his Women. But the warriors began shooting at him. He was having a hard time with so many Persons after him, and he cried: "Help me — help me, why don't you?"

Oh, ho! Skinkoots began shooting so fast

that his arrows made those Persons stop. "Now you let that Bull-person have his Women," he told the warriors. And they had to do that.

When they were far away from the village the Bull said: "I will give you one of these Women. Take your choice. You are my friend."

Skinkoots picked out the younger. Then he said to himself: "I think she looks as though she would be tough. I had better choose the other one." And he changed, of course, and the Bull let him take the other one.

"Well, I guess I shall go back now," said Skinkoots, leaving the Bull to go his own way.

When he was far away from there Skinkoots said: "Now, Woman, you go around this hill *this* way, and I will cross over it *that* way."

The Woman started, and Skinkoots ran over the hill and sat down on a rock to wait for her to come along. It was a big hill, and he waited and waited. He sat very still till at last the Woman came along. Then he shot her dead. Oh, ho! He killed that Woman dead!

But even then he did not move. He just sat there and looked, till the Wolf-person came along and commenced to eat his dead Buffalo-woman.

"Hey, you! Go away from here! Kill your own meat!" called Skinkoots. "Go away, or I will —" He tried to get up. He tried to move from the rock, and could not. Oh, ho! He was stuck fast to the rock! It held him!

He called the Wolf-person names. But the Wolf ate and ate until only the bones were left. Oh, ho! Nothing was left but the bones.

"Well," said Skinkoots when the Wolf-person went away from there, "I can get along with those bones. I will break them and eat the marrow, if I can get off this rock."

He pulled *hard* and he came off. "Well, this is funny," he said. "I pulled harder than that before." But he had *not* pulled hard. He was afraid of the Wolf-person and he had not pulled very hard while the Wolf was there.

He ran to the bones. "Oh, ho!" he said, and

picked up a big bone with which to break the others.

"Wait! Wait! Do not do that!" Some Person was talking.

"*Something is going on here,* I guess," said Skinkoots, looking around. Then he saw the Badger-person coming along.

"Let me do that for you, Skinkoots," said the Badger, coming up.

"No, I will not," said Skinkoots. And he grabbed Badger's tail. That is why the Badger's tail is so queer, even to this day. Skinkoots broke off a piece of Badger's tail!

Then to make Badger glad again Skinkoots said: "I will run you a race for these bones."

But the Badger beat him. Oh, ho! The Badger beat Skinkoots and ate about all the marrow there was in those bones.

"Well, anyway, I can boil what is left, and drink the soup," sighed Skinkoots. "I will get at it before somebody else comes along."

"Wait! Wait! Do not do that! Let me, let me!"

Skinkoots looked around, and saw the Blue Jay-person.

"What can *you* do?" he asked the Bird-person, gathering up the scraps of bone.

"If you will go and gather some good roots I will make us a lot of soup with these bones," said the Blue Jay-person, hopping around there.

"All right," said Skinkoots. But when he came back with his roots all was gone! Oh, ho! Not a scrap was left. The Blue Jay-person had finished the bones.

Ho!

XIV

THE STORY OF LITTLE ROCK

NOW I will tell you about Little Rock. He lived with his father and mother, and they were old.

One day when his father was out hunting, Little Rock said to his mother: "Are there no more People around here?"

"No. There are no others around here," answered his mother, "but there are other People far away, and some of them are Persons."

"I guess I will go and find them," said Little Rock.

But his mother said: "No. Your father's gone now. Wait until he returns, and hear what he says about it."

When his father returned, his mother told him what their son, Little Rock, had said.

"Well, if you wish to go it is all right," he told

Little Rock. "But it is very far off, and you will be afraid many times."

So Little Rock, who was young and handsome, went out of his father's lodge. He travelled very far through the forests, came to big rivers and crossed them, walked where the way was pleasant, and in country that was rough, until he came to the mountains. Then he began to climb. Near the top he looked down and saw a Person coming up the hill.

He stood still, watching the Person until the Person stopped and looked up at him. Then Little Rock knew who he was.

"I see Little Rock," said the Person, starting up again.

"I see Badger," said Little Rock, wondering if he ought to wait there.

In no time at all Badger was beside him.

"Where did you come from?" he asked.

"Oh, not far away," answered the Badger. "I live on this hill, and I stay at home most of the time. Where are you going?"

"I am looking for the Other People."

"Oh, you are? Well, they are very far off, I can tell you. You will come to big mountains, and when you climb them you will see more mountains. And when you climb these you will see more mountains, and when you climb these — well, maybe you will see the village of the Other People — *maybe*."

"Well, I guess I will be going," said Little Rock. "Ho!"

"Wait," said Badger. "I guess I had just as soon go with you. I used to live over there."

Little Rock did not like that talk. He was a little afraid. But he thought it would be all right if Badger went along, and so they began travelling together.

Badger's clothes were pretty. But Little Rock wore a robe of painted Elk-skin that was handsome, and Badger liked it. He even spoke of it that day to Little Rock.

They came to big mountains, and when they climbed them they saw more mountains. And when they climbed these they saw more mountains. And when they had climbed these they saw the village of the Other People. But it was far off.

"That is the place," said Badger. "But we must be careful how we go from here."

They cut brush to carry before them, and crept down to a hill where they could see all the lodges in the village. Many were painted; and some were white, and some were black lodges. All were very still.

Little Rock and Badger lay down behind the bushes they carried, so that if People looked up there they would see only the bushes.

"I see the Chief's lodge," said Badger. "I know that Chief. He is Cas-pi-ooks, the Sandhill Crane-person, and he has a pretty daughter who never goes out of that lodge when there are any Persons around there. This is because she does not want to be married. But every night she comes alone to this hill. I wish we could catch her to-night when she comes here."

149

When the night came Badger said: "Hold my robe, Little Rock, while I find a better place to see. Do not drop it. If you do we shall have bad luck."

He had heard somebody walking, and wished to load his friend down so that he could not run very fast. That is why he gave his robe to Little Rock. But Little Rock had not heard the walking, and took Badger's robe.

In no time at all the Girl was there. Both ran after her. But Badger caught her. He had nothing to carry, and he caught the Girl and held her till Little Rock came and made him let go.

Then in no time at all the Girl was gone. But she had seen Little Rock's Elk-skin robe. Badger knew she had seen it, and he knew she liked it, too.

"Now we shall have to go down there," said Badger, pretending he was not angry at Little Rock.

"Here," he said, "your robe is heavy. Let

150

me carry it, and you carry mine." And so they crept into the village with Little Rock wearing Badger's robe and Badger wearing Little Rock's robe of painted Elk-skin.

"I will go in first and see how I get along," whispered Badger, when they were beside the Chief's lodge. Softly he opened the door and walked in.

The Girl thought he was Little Rock, and looked glad. She took hold of Badger's arm — oh, ho! — then she struck him in the nose! That is why Badger's nose turns up even to this day.

Badger began to fight the Girl, but she whipped him, and he ran out of there.

"I guess she must want you. She will not have me," he said to Little Rock, handing him his Elk-skin robe.

Little Rock walked into that lodge and put his arm around that Girl, and she did not even pinch him. Then he came out and said to Badger: "I am going to marry that Girl now."

"Well, let us find something to eat first," said Badger. "I know an Old Woman in this village who will feed us. Then if you want that Girl you can take her. I do not care."

The Old Woman was a Frog. "What do you two want here?" she asked when Badger led the way into her lodge. "You will be killed if you stay around this place," she said. But she gave them some food.

"We are going to be careful, Old Woman," said Badger. "When do Persons get married here?"

"Oh, in the morning," said the Old Frog-woman. "In the morning."

"We had better be careful here," advised Badger. "You must wait until morning. Besides, we must dress ourselves for this thing."

Little Rock knew the Girl was waiting, and he tried to hurry, but always Badger had to change the paint on his face, or fix something until it was morning.

Then they went to the lodge of Cas-pi-oots,

the Sand-hill Crane-person — and the Girl was gone! Oh, ho! Nobody knew where she was. She had grown tired of waiting, and she had run away. Oh, ho! Nobody knew where she had gone!

The Chief sent all his People to look for her. They went to the Big Salty Water, and *Sinna*, the Beaver, swam far out.

"Go back to our village," he told all the People. "To-morrow I will find the daughter of Cas-pi-oots and bring her to his lodge."

"Good," said all the People, and they went back to their village. But that night a big storm came on the Salty Water, and Beaver had to give it up. He came alone to the village the next morning.

Now Little Rock's heart was on the ground. He went to the Old Frog-woman. "Will you help me find that Girl, Old Woman?" he begged her. "If you will find her I will give you my clothes."

"Oh, I do not want your clothes, but if I am

going to travel so far, I *do* want your paint,"
said the Old Frog-woman.

"Here, take it!" said Little Rock.

And then the Old Frog-woman painted her
legs and painted her back, and spotted herself
very prettily — she is that way to this day, and
now you know why.

"Come," she said, and they went to the Big
Salty Water together, with Badger trailing along
behind to see what was going on.

"Now you sit here," said the Old Frog-
woman, spreading a robe by the Salty Water.

Little Rock and Badger sat down there, and
the Old Frog-woman went into the Big Salty
Water. "I will be back with that Girl to-
morrow at this time," she said from a white
wave.

Little Rock and Badger sat on that robe all
night. But the Old Frog-woman had to go to
the middle of the Big Salty Water, and besides
there came a bad storm, so that she had a hard
time out there.

But just at the time she said she would bring the Girl, Little Rock saw her coming away out where there were big waves. And she was dragging something.

When she got to the shore, she beckoned. "Do not speak," she told them, when Little Rock and Badger had come to her. "Take this thing to my lodge."

The thing was a Big White Rock. Badger took hold of it, but he could not move it.

Little Rock pushed him back, and picked up the Big White Rock.

"Follow me, but do not speak," said the Old Frog-woman. And at last Little Rock carried the Big White Rock into the Old Frog-woman's lodge and put it down there.

"Now sit up and watch it. But do not speak. No matter what happens there must be no talking here," said the Old Frog-woman. Then she went to sleep, because she was tired.

Little Rock and Badger put sticks on the fire many times. But they did not speak. Midnight came and they had not spoken. Then a Girl's arm came out of the Big White Rock, slowly, slowly!

Badger grabbed it.

"Let — go — let go," cried Little Rock.

Oh, ho! The arm was gone. No arm was there. Only the Big White Rock was there!

Morning came, and night came, and midnight came. Then a Girl's *head* came slowly, slowly, out of the Big White Rock. Her eyes smiled upon Little Rock, and his heart sang.

"Keep quiet now," he whispered.

And oh, ho! The Girl's *head* was gone! There was no Girl's *head* there! Only the Big White Rock was with them in the lodge!

Morning came again, and night, and then midnight. A Girl began coming slowly, slowly, slowly out of the Big White Rock. The fire crackled, and *Co*-pee, the Owl, spoke, but this time Little Rock and Badger kept still.

Slowly, slowly, with smiling eyes that looked at Little Rock, the Girl came out farther and farther until she stepped upon the ground. Then she put her arms around Little Rock. And they danced together.

Ho!

XV

STEALING THE SPRINGTIME

"THE snows will soon come," said Two-comes-over-the-hill, looking gravely at the sparkling lodge-fire. "But the Winter does not last as it once did. I will tell you why. Of course Skinkoots had a hand in what happened to change the Seasons. It was Skinkoots who started it all. And we are glad he did, for now the Summer stays with us six Moons.

"Listen! The snow was deep. It bent the trees. It covered the ice on the lakes until they looked like parks in the forest. Every Person was thin, even those who store up food for the Winter. The busiest of these could not gather enough food during the short Summer to last him through the long Winter.

"Skinkoots was walking on his snow-shoes.

He was hungry, and asked at every lodge for something to eat. At last he came to the lodge of an Old Woman. This Old Woman was the Pine Squirrel-person, and she gave him some food. The food was wild-rose hips which she had gathered during the Summer-time. She did not have many left, and she cried when Skinkoots ate the last one.

"'Oh, dear, what can I do? It will not be Spring for a long time. I shall die!' she wailed.

"'What is that you are saying?' asked Skinkoots, licking his chops.

"'I said there is no more food and it is Winter. I shall starve. Oh, what shall I do?'

"'Do? Why, cry, of course! Cry hard! And when the Persons come here and ask you why you cry, do not answer them. Just keep on crying. Finally I will come in and ask: "Do you say there will be no more food for a long time?" And you must say: "Yes."'

"Skinkoots went out of the lodge and the Old Woman began to cry. Persons came to her lodge and asked: 'Why do you cry?' But she would not answer them. She just kept on crying, crying, crying, until in came Skinkoots.

"'What is going on here?' he asked of all the Persons there.

"'This Old Woman is crying, and she will not tell us why she cries. That is all,' answered somebody, across the fire.

"'Say, you,' said Skinkoots, looking at the Old Woman, 'do you say there will be no more food until Spring?'

"'Yes,' wailed the Old Woman, 'that is what I said. What shall we do to bring back the Springtime?'

"'Well, I will see about this,' said Skinkoots, and went out of the Old Woman's lodge.

"There was a village of many lodges. It was far away and strong. The Persons who lived there kept the Summer-time tied up in a Moose-skin bag. They kept all the Seasons that way. They used to untie the Winter and let him stay out twelve months sometimes. This was because they liked him best. But so much Winter made it hard for the other Persons, and something had to be done about it.

"Skinkoots knew about all this, and he travelled steadily until he had found the Softest-walker, and the Farthest-thrower, and the Strongest-one among all the Persons he knew. He said to them: 'The Springtime is in a Moose-skin bag that hangs in the Chief's lodge over that way.' And he pointed North. 'Let us go and steal that bag and untie it. But we must not get hold of the wrong one, for there are three bags hanging there. We must steal the bag that holds the Springtime and not make a mistake, or we shall mix things.'

"'Good,' said the Grizzly Bear. 'I shall have a hard time travelling. I am so sleepy and heavy. But I will help you. Lead on.'

"'Yes,' said Skinkoots, 'you are the Strongest-person. Your Medicine is powerful. Come with us.'

"And so these four started for the strange village. All the other Persons followed to learn what was going on.

"At last they came to the village. It was nearly hidden by the deep snow, and looked bad under the stars.

"'Hey, you Persons, hide yourselves on that hill,' said Skinkoots, beckoning the Grizzly Bear and the Softest-walker and the Farthest-thrower to come to him.

"'See that big lodge?' asked Skinkoots, pointing to a big black tepee with white smoke coming from its top.

"'Yes, we see it,' said the Grizzly Bear and the Softest-walker and the Farthest-thrower, craning their necks and pricking up their ears.

"'Well, that is it,' said Skinkoots, 'and you must be careful. Listen! There will be an Old Woman in that lodge. She is a loud talker, and you must be careful not to let her talk much. Remember this.

"'Here, Softest-walker, take this pitch, and

when you get inside sit by the lodge-fire and pretend to warm your hands, but melt the pitch; melt the pitch in your hand. When the pitch is soft and very sticky you must ask: "Where is the Springtime, Old Woman?"

"'She will say, "It is hanging there," and point to the bag. Then you must stop her mouth with the hot pitch and hold it there until it sticks *tight*. Then the Old Woman will not be able to speak. The hot pitch will stop her words. When you have done this, take down the bag that holds the Springtime and throw it outside. Have you listened?'

"'Yes,' answered Softest-walker, 'I have listened.'

"'Now *you*, Farthest-thrower, listen to me,' said Skinkoots, speaking fast. 'When this Person throws that bag outside the lodge, you grab it. Grab it quick! And throw it far; farther than you ever threw a thing before. Throw it over that way.' And he pointed to the hill where the other Persons were hiding. 'Well, that is your job,' said Skinkoots. 'Have you listened, Farthest-thrower?'

"'Yes,' answered Farthest-thrower, 'I have listened.'

"'And now *you*, Strongest-one,' he said to the Grizzly Bear, 'go over there on that hill among the others. When the bag comes you catch it. Catch it and *tear* it! Tear it *bad*, and tear it *quickly!* That is all you have to do. Have you listened, Strongest-one?'

"'Yes,' answered Grizzly Bear-person, 'I have listened.'

"'Well, then get at your jobs. I will be over there to watch what is going on. Now be careful, all of you. And remember my words!'

"Softest-walker went to the lodge and slipped inside with the ball of pitch in his hand. He did not make a sound in his walking.

"Farthest-thrower sat down on the snow piled up by the door. He could hear all that went on inside, too. And he listened.

"Softest-walker sat down by the fire and held

164

his hands over it. Yes, he held them where the ball of pitch would get hot.

"'The weather is cold, Old Woman,' he said, looking up at the three bags hanging on the lodge-poles.

"'Yes, it is,' she answered, without even looking at him.

"The pitch was growing soft now. It was pretty sticky already, so Softest-walker asked: 'Where is the Springtime, Old Woman?'

"'That is it, hanging over your head,' she answered, pointing to the bag.

"Swow! Softest-walker stopped the Old Woman's mouth with the hot pitch, and held it there!

"Oh, ho! She tried to speak! She tried to scream! But the hot pitch stuck tight and held back her words, just as Skinkoots had said it would. She tried to run outside, but Softest-walker pushed her back and grabbed the bag.

"Oh, ho! He grabbed the bag! The Old Woman threw her arms around him, but he managed to shake her off, and toss the bag out through the door, where Strongest-thrower was waiting for it.

"Oh, ho! He grabbed it! Lifted it high and threw it! Up — up it went, and over the other lodges.

"Both Softest-walker and Farthest-thrower saw it sail to the hill as they ran away after it. They saw Grizzly Bear catch the bag and tear it open, felt the soft Winds touching their faces, even before they reached their friends on the hillside. Oh, ho! It was *Springtime!*

"The snow was melting by the time Softest-walker and Farthest-thrower caught up with the other Persons, who were running away with the Springtime.

"Ho!"